GW00374135

Wishing you a
FABULOUS CHRISTMAS
and an even better
NEW YEAR from all of the
team at
MILLS & BOON®

£5.99

afternoon delight
Carol Marinelli

'Alice!'

The familiar voice of her husband shouting over to her caused Alice to literally freeze on the spot, cursing herself for her lack of foresight – it hadn't even entered her head that she'd run into Declan. A pretty stupid detail to overlook, given that he worked near Southbank and every Friday went out with his colleagues for lunch there!

'Declan.' Alice forced a smile as, leaving the clique of grey suits he was walking with, navy eyes squinting against the sun, dark hair flopping over his forehead, he made his way over. The curious smile on his face coupled with a frown.

'What are you doing here?'

She could feel his eyes as they drifted over her, and felt horribly exposed as she stood on the hotel steps, a good couple of feet higher than him. Alice knew he was taking in every detail – noticing how her normally non-descript brown curly hair fell for once in a sleek glossy curtain, courtesy of the fabulous ceramic straighteners he'd bought her for her last birthday. She knew that Declan was wondering what the hell she was doing in the city on a Friday lunchtime, made up to the nines, swathed in her favourite dress and strappy sandals. And she also knew that she couldn't tell him the truth.

'I can't tell you!' Alice watched as the curious smile faded, his frown deepening

as he stared back at her, and she forced herself to smile as she looked him in the eye and lied, 'I can't tell you because it's supposed to be a surprise.'

'A surprise?'

One of his colleagues was calling him, and Declan gave him a brief wave, called over that he'd be there in a minute, then stared back at his wife, who was supposed to be safely tucked up in suburbia, dropping the twins off at nursery or walking the treadmill at the gym.

'Alice, what the hell's going on?'

'If I tell you, I'll spoil the surprise!' Alice gave what she hoped was a mysterious smile and glanced nervously over to his colleagues, who were getting impatient now, no doubt eager to get in a few glasses of wine with their lunch. 'They're waiting for you.'

'I don't give a damn...' Declan started, but Alice halted him.

'Please, Declan, don't spoil this. Ring me on my mobile when you leave the office – just pretend that you didn't see me. It will be worth it, I promise.'

She knew she hadn't mollified him in the slightest, but for now at least he bought it. Kissing him goodbye, Alice felt a horrible stab of guilt for the rotten afternoon Declan would have now, the hundred and one questions that would surely be racing around in his mind till he saw her again.

Then panic took over – now she had to come up with a suitable surprise!

'Debbie, I know it's horribly short notice,' Alice mumbled into her mobile as she handed over her credit card to the hotel receptionist, 'but can you pick up the twins from nursery for me?'

'Sure,' her friend replied easily. Alice closed her eyes and winced.

'And possibly have them stay for a sleep-over?'

'Tonight!'

'Please.' Alice gulped. 'I hate to ask. It's just...'

And out it all came – how Declan had caught her on the hotel steps, how she'd had to think fast on her high-heeled feet, and how a night in a luxury hotel was the only thing she'd been able to come up with.

'Okay, fine.' Debbie gave a rather martyred sigh, and frankly Alice couldn't blame her. The twins were certainly double the trouble at the best of times. 'But, Alice, what are you doing in the city?' When Alice didn't immediately answer, and all that came down the crackling phone line was silence, Debbie guessed the truth in a moment.

'You were going to see Dave, weren't you? Oh, Alice, what is it with that guy?

I just don't know what you see in him – he's so up himself, so opinionated...'

'I just wanted to say goodbye properly to him.'

Alice ran an exasperated hand through her hair, knowing that no matter what she said now, Debbie would never understand how she felt about Dave.

Alice had never intended to ring him – his hastily jotted down number had lain, half forgotten and occasionally remembered, in the bottom of her bag for weeks. But one afternoon when the kids were at nursery, when Declan had rung and told her not to worry about dinner because he was eating out with clients, when the house was spotless and she couldn't face the gym again, she had taken the scrappy piece of paper out of her bag.

Scarcely believing her own actions, she'd picked up the phone and dialled his number. Admittedly she'd been tempted to slam down the phone when he'd answered, but faltering, blushing, she'd stammered out an introduction. He must have sensed her nervousness, realised that perhaps this wasn't something Alice usually did, because he'd taken things very gently with her. In his own unique way, he put her at ease – told her something funny that had made her giggle, then finished things off by adding that she had a beautiful laugh. A cliché to end all clichés, but Dave, as Debbie frequently pointed out, was full of them.

'Why don't you just buy a book of quotations?' Debbie had snorted one day, when the two women had been sitting around the kitchen table as Alice brought her friend up to date with all that was happening. 'We all know that life is too short for regrets, and we all want to follow our hearts and live for the moment – the only trouble is Dave seems to forget that you've got four-year-old twins, a husband and a mortgage. It doesn't exactly leave much room for spontaneity. I'm sick of hearing about Dave!'

'What's all this?' A slow, lazy smile inched over Declan's mouth as he walked into the stunning hotel room, taking in the massive arrangement of fresh flowers, the champagne chilling in the bucket – and Alice, wearing nothing more than a nervous smile, lying propped up on one elbow on the bed.

'Your surprise.' Alice gulped, feeling cold and stupid and a million miles from spontaneous. But Dave had told her once that this was exactly the sort of thing a man liked – and to stop worrying about her stretch marks because he could guarantee that he wasn't!

'No twins?' Declan grinned.

'They're at Debbie's.'

'For how long?'

'Till tomorrow.' Alice gulped again, realizing that for Declan that was probably

the biggest surprise of them all. He knew how much she hated leaving them with anyone. Well, actually she loved leaving them – it was the hefty dose of guilt that came when you landed a friend with two hyperactive, fabulously boisterous four-year-olds. That was the bit Alice hated.

'Oh, Alice.' Sitting down on the bed beside her, he took her in his arms, held onto her for the longest time and groaned into her hair. 'You've no idea of the afternoon I've had – I was half expecting to walk in here and hear you tell me we were finished.'

'Finished?' Alice gave a low laugh and started taking off his tie. 'We haven't even started...'

'You are happy, aren't you?' Declan asked ages later, when the champagne had long since gone and the tiny bottle of bath gel had been well and truly used up.

Lying on the bed, draped in a fluffy white robe, Alice didn't hesitate before answering.

'Very.'

'But you haven't been.' Declan gazed down at her with worried eyes. 'For the last few months you've been...' He struggled to find the right word, and Alice finished his sentence for him.

'Thinking.' Alice smiled. 'I've been doing a lot of thinking.'

'About?'

'Me.'

'Us?' Declan checked, but Alice shook her head.

'We're fine,' Alice said assuredly. 'It's just...' Not so assuredly she stumbled on. 'Well, the twins will be at school next year, and as much as I've loved being a stay-at-home mum...'

'You want to go back to work?'

Again she shook her head. 'I want to go back to school, Declan. You know how much I enjoy helping out at the nursery? Well, I was speaking to the teacher, and she said that with my qualifications I should have no trouble getting in. She's more than happy to give me a reference...'

'You want to be a nursery teacher?' A smile twitched on his face. 'You don't look like a nursery school teacher, Alice.'

'So, what does one look like?'

'Matronly?' Declan shrugged, but Alice just laughed.

'Maybe when you were a boy. But that was last century...' Her laughter faded, her eyes pleading with him to take her seriously. 'I really want to do it, Declan. I know it won't be easy, that we'll have to juggle–'

'Do it, then,' Declan broke in. 'If that's what you want to do, Alice, then go for it!'

As easily as that, he accepted it. Alice blinked at the simplicity of it all, wondering why it had taken so many months of soul-searching and angst to tell him what she really wanted out of life.

Because she hadn't known what she wanted, Alice realised, lying back on the bed, watching as Declan wandered around the hotel room checking out the view and the contents of the mini-bar.

Pouring her a glass of Bailey's, he joined her back on the bed, and because he was a man, and there was a remote control handy, in a reflex action he flicked on the television. Alice lay back on the pillow and gazed at the ceiling. When she'd first rung Dave, all those months ago, all Alice had known was that there had to be more – that when the twins started school, an extra aerobics class, or even starting back at her old office, wasn't going to be enough to fill her days, fill her life. It had been Dave who had held her hand as she'd explored her options. Dave who'd told her she could be whatever she wanted to be if only she put her mind to it.

And today she'd finally said thank you.

'Talk about *Desperate Housewives*...' Declan's white terry-towelled elbow nudged her out of her daydream.

'Look at this lot, Alice!'

Face paling, Alice watched the news bulletin – watched as the reporter told of how two hundred women had descended on a Southbank hotel today to say farewell to their favourite talkback radio host. How Dave Bailey had put on a champagne reception for his lovely ladies before he left Australia to follow his own dreams and move to the United States with his latest boyfriend.

'How can a man who doesn't even like women claim to know what they really want?' Declan scoffed. 'How many did they say turned out to see him?'

'Two hundred, I think,' Alice answered faintly, breathing a sigh of relief as the story ended and the reporter started to address the weather. 'Or was it two hundred and one?' she mumbled with a satisfied smile as Declan picked up the phone to order room service, realising that she'd actually got away with it.

Never in a million years would Declan guess her real reason for being in the city that afternoon. It would never even enter his head that for a few months there his own wife had been a talkback radio addict, listening to Dave's little pearls of wisdom...

Every weekday afternoon, between twelve and three! ▪

If you love medical TV programmes – then why not try a Medical Romance™? The Surgeon's Miracle Baby by CAROL MARINELLI is on sale in January.

Deck the
& the Living

When it comes to the holidays nothing is more fun than pulling out your box of ornaments, candles and sentimental treasures. Christmas baubles packed tightly in tissue, hand-made family crafts from years ago buried on the bottom and often your tree angel tucked in on top. As you get ready to decorate this year, why not try some of our tips to help give you some added festive flair!

Here's how to get started. It may be time to re-evaluate your treasures. If your fairy lights look like a blinking ball of string with fruit-punch-coloured lights intertwined, it's time to move on to simple white lights. A few strands of soft white fairy lights are a stunning basis to any style of décor, and quite honestly, they look fabulous all year long – throw them on a potted plant or wrap them around a branch in your garden when you are done.

That way, you don't have to spend hours de-tangling them next year.

Building and layering is the key to any décor scheme regardless of the season. Once you have a chosen a theme and a colour scheme (say red and white), mix your old favourites with some newer ornaments to keep the space fresh. Remember to continue the theme throughout, from the tree to your dining room table and the flower arrangements. A unified look is what you're after. So, follow these decorating tips to a stunning seasonal space for the Christmas holidays.

GO NATURAL

Fresh evergreens not only add a fantastic smell to the house, but they are a simple way of decorating. All you need to enhance them are some clear or white frosted lights or a few votive candles tucked in between the bows. Also, try mixing in a few pinecones and branches for more of an earthy effect.

Halls
Room, Too!
by Tanya Linton

BE CREATIVE WITH A CENTREPIECE

Release your inner decorator. Think of new ideas for the table. Try gathering pillar candles of multi-heights and lay them on a baking tray and tuck mounds of moss and cranberries in between. Or throw a combination of citrus fruits in a bowl (like oranges, clementines and kumquats) with greenery and cranberries.

COLOUR COMBOS

It's important to pick a holiday colour scheme so that you can create an overall theme. Go for two colours and be as inventive as you like. Red and green is traditional, red and white is more sophisticated and unusual combinations like icy blue and chocolate brown are a contemporary take. It's okay to add a splash of extra colour to jazz up your scheme like dots of pink flowers against a red and white room or white accessories paired with a red and green scheme. Although, limit your look to just one additional colour.

WRAP IT UP

Make your friends and family savour the outside as much as the gift inside with creative ideas for Christmas wrapping. Take-away containers, wallpaper scraps, even newspaper make for unique statements, especially topped with gorgeous ribbon. Just like the decorating theme, it's helpful to have a wrapping plan of attack – complete with colour choices, complementary ribbons and pretty tie-able tags.

FORBIDDEN FRUITS

Who says that you can't decorate with fresh fruit? Clementines, pears, apples, pomegranates and kumquats all make for beautiful statements. Whether tucked into a wreath, scattered across a mantelpiece or simply piled high in a clear glass bowl as a centrepiece, fresh fruit is less perishable and more economical than flowers.

IT'S OKAY TO BE REPETITIVE

The easiest way to make a décor statement in your home is with repetition. Try placing a row of white votive candles on your mantelpiece alternating with a shiny rustic apple. Or line the centre of your dining room table with a row of pomegranates. The key is to use odd numbers – three or five works best.

FLICKERING LIGHT

Natural light makes all the difference (and it's most flattering!) so gather up all of your votives and scatter throughout. Try keeping your candle colours unified – all white or all red or limit it to two colours.

Here's a fun and easy project that will add some welcoming holiday cheer to your home but won't take a weekend to do. Feel free to use non-citrus fruits, but keep in mind that the larger the fruit, the heavier the wreath will be.

Citrus Holiday Wreath Project

Materials and tools required:

- 1 fresh round or square boxwood wreath available at your local flower shop (fake versions can be found at craft supply stores).

- A strip of ribbon, two inches wide – colour your choice.

- 20 kumquats (try clementines or limes as well).

- 2 branches of inedible berries (there are a ton of varieties at your local flower shop but you could also use clusters of sewn cranberries).

- 1 roll of florist wire.

- 1 pair of scissors.

This wreath is a wonderful addition to the festive period. To make this citrus wreath, lay your boxwood wreath on a newspaper covered table. Roughly judge the placement of the citrus fruit, scattering them all over. Spear the kumquats with wire from top to bottom (if they still are attached to leaves, even better – just wrap the wire around the branches) and wrap tightly around the boxwood frame. Once you have wired all of the kumquats in place, finish the wreath by stuffing the bare areas with berry branches. Finally, wrap the ribbon a few times at the top of the wreath and allow enough left over to create a floppy loop for hanging. Once you are done, test it out on the front door.

SU DOKU

To solve a **Su Doku** puzzle fill in all the squares in the grid so that each row, column and each of the 3x3 'inner squares' contains the numbers 1 to 9.

		8		3				
				4		9	2	3
	3							4
3		4	5	8	6		1	9
8	9		1	7	2	4	3	
5	1	1	4	9	3	5		
		7					9	
1	8		7				4	
				5	4	7	6	2

KAKURO

To solve a **Kakuro** fill the grid with numbers so that each block of spaces adds up to the total in the box above or to the left of it. You can only use the digits 1-9 and you must not use the same digit twice in a single block of spaces. (The same digit may occur more than once in a row or column, but it must be in a separate block.)

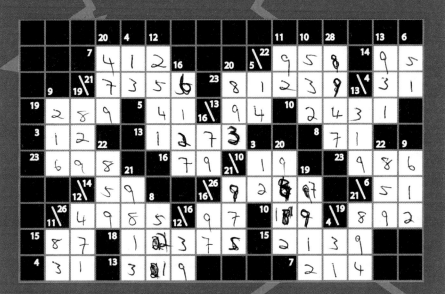

**The two men talking together
at the back of the hospital
entrance hall paused to watch a
young woman cross the vast floor.**
She was walking briskly, which suggested
that she knew just where she was going,
but she paused for a moment to speak to
one of the porters and they had the chance
to study her at their leisure.

She was worth studying: a quantity of
dark brown hair framed a beautiful face
and the nylon overall she was wearing
couldn't disguise her splendid figure.

'Eulalia Langley,' said the elder of the two
men, 'runs the canteen in Outpatients.

Good at it, too. Lives with her grandfather,
old Colonel Langley—your father knew
him, Aderik. No money, lives in a splendid
house somewhere behind Cheyne Walk.
Some family arrangement makes it
impossible for him to sell it—has to pass it
on to a nephew. A millstone round his
neck; Eulalia lives with him, keeps the
home going. She's been with us for several
years now. Ought to have married by now
but I don't suppose there's much chance
of that. It's a full-time job here and there
isn't much of the day left by the time the
canteen shuts down.'

His companion said quietly, 'She's very

beautiful,' and then added, 'You say that my father knew Colonel Langley?'

He watched the girl go on her way and then turned to his companion. He was tall and heavily built, and towered over his informative colleague. A handsome man in his thirties, he had pale hair already streaked with grey, a high-bridged nose above a thin mouth and heavy-lidded blue eyes. His voice held only faint interest.

'Yes—during the Second World War. They saw a good deal of each other over the years. I don't think you ever met him? Peppery man, and I gather from what I hear that he is housebound with severe arthritis and is now even more peppery.'

'Understandably. Shall I see more of you before I go back to Holland?'

'I hope you'll find time to come to dinner; Dora will want to see you and ask after your mother. You're going to Edinburgh this evening?'

'Yes, but I should be back here tomorrow—I'm operating and there's an Outpatient clinic I must fit in before I return.'

'Then I'll give you a ring.'

The older man smiled. 'You are making quite a name for yourself, Aderik, just as your father did.'

Eulalia, unaware of this conversation, went on her way through the hospital to the Outpatients department, already filling up for the morning clinic.

It was a vast place, with rows of wooden benches and noisy old-fashioned radiators which did little to dispel the chill of early winter. Although a good deal of St Chad's had been brought up to date, and that in the teeth of official efforts to close it, there wasn't enough money to spend on the department so its walls remained that particular green so beloved by authority, its benches scuffed and stained and its linoleum floor, once green like the walls, now faded to no colour at all.

Whatever its shortcomings, they were greatly mitigated by the canteen counter which occupied the vast wall, covered in cheerful plastic and nicely set out with piles of plates, cups and saucers, soup mugs, spoons, knives and paper serviettes.

Eulalia saw with satisfaction that Sue and Polly were filling the tea urn and the sugar bowls. The first of the patients were already coming in although the first clinic wouldn't open for another hour, but Outpatients, for all its drawbacks, was for many of the patients a sight better than cold bedsitters and loneliness.

Eulalia had seen that from the first moment of starting her job and since then, for four years, she had fought, splendid white tooth and nail, for the small comforts which would turn the unwelcoming place into somewhere in which the hours of waiting could be borne in some degree of comfort.

Since there had been no money to

modernise the place, she had concentrated on the canteen, turning it by degrees into a buffet serving cheap, filling food, soup and drinks, served in brightly coloured crockery by cheerful, chatty helpers.

With an eye on the increasing flow of patients, she sent two of the girls to coffee and went to check the soup. The early morning clinic was chests, and that meant any number of elderly people who lived in damp and chilly rooms and never had quite enough to eat. Soup, even so early in the morning, would be welcome, washed down by strong tea...

One clinic succeeded another; frequently two or more ran consecutively, but by six o'clock the place was silent. Eulalia, after doing a last careful check, locked up, handed over the keys to the head porter and went home.

It was a long journey across the city but the first surge of home-goers had left so she had a seat in the bus and she walked for the last ten minutes or so, glad of the exercise, making her way through the quieter streets down towards the river until she reached a terrace of imposing houses in a narrow, tree-lined street.

Going up the steps to a front door, she glanced down at the basement. The curtains were drawn but she could see that there was a light there, for Jane would be getting supper. Eulalia put her key in the door and opened the inner door to the hall, lighted by a lamp on a side table—a handsome marble-topped nineteenth-century piece which, sadly, her grandfather was unable to sell since it was all part and parcel of the family arrangement...

There was a rather grand staircase at the end of the hall and doors on either side, but she passed them and went through the green baize door at the end of the hall and down the small staircase to the basement.

The kitchen was large with a large old-fashioned dresser along one wall, a scrubbed table at its centre and a Rayburn cooker, very much the worse for wear. But it was warm and something smelled delicious.

Eulalia wrinkled her beautiful nose. 'Toad-in-the-hole? Roasted onions?'

The small round woman peeling apples at the table turned to look at her.

'There you are, Miss Lally. The kettle's on the boil; I'll make you a nice cup of tea in a couple of shakes. The Colonel had his two hours ago.'

'I'll take a cup of tea with me, Jane; he'll be wanting his whisky. Then I'll come and give you a hand.'

She poured her own tea, and put a mug beside Jane. 'Has Grandfather had a good day?'

'He had a letter that upset him, Miss Lally.' Jane's nice elderly face looked worried. 'You know how it is; something bothers him and he gets that upset.'

'I'll go and sit with him for a bit.' Eulalia swallowed the rest of her tea, paused to stroke Dickens, the cat, asleep by the stove, and made her way upstairs.

The Colonel had a room on the first floor of the house at the front. It was a handsome apartment furnished with heavy mahogany pieces of the Victorian period. They had been his grandparents' and although the other rooms were furnished mostly with Regency pieces, he loved the solid bulk of wardrobe, dressing table and vast tallboy.

He was sitting in his chair by the gas fire, reading, when she tapped on the door and went in.

He turned his bony old face with its formidable nose towards her and put his book down. 'Lally— just in time to pour my whisky. Come and sit down and tell me about your day.'

She gave him his drink and sat down on a cross-framed stool, its tapestry almost threadbare, and gave him a light-hearted account of it, making much of its lighter moments. But although he chuckled from time to time he was unusually silent, so that presently she asked, 'Something's wrong, Grandfather?'

'Nothing for you to worry your pretty head about, Lally. Stocks and shares aren't a woman's business and it is merely a temporary setback.'

Lally murmured soothingly. Grandfather belonged to the generation which considered that women had nothing to do with a man's world, and it was rather late in the day to argue with him about that.

She said cheerfully into the little silence, 'Jane and I were only saying this morning that it was a waste of gas and electricity keeping the drawing room open. I never go in there, and if anyone comes to call we can use the morning room...'

'I'll not have you living in the kitchen,' said the Colonel tetchily.

> **CHRISTMAS TIP**
> Make your Christmas party stand out from the rest by giving your guests a "good luck" gift bag. You can fill them with a whole range of things—chocolates, sweets, mini bottles of their favourite drinks, or perhaps flower seeds to brighten up the garden in the New Year.

'Well, of course not,' agreed Lally cheerfully, and thought how easy it was to tell fibs once she got started. 'But you must agree that the drawing room takes a lot of time to get warm even with the central heating on all day. We could cut it down for a few hours.'

He agreed reluctantly and she heaved a sigh of relief. The drawing room had been unheated for weeks and so, in fact, had most of the rooms in the house; only her grandfather's room was warm, as was the small passage leading to an equally warm bathroom. Lally wasn't deceitful but needs must when the devil drove...

She went back to the kitchen presently and ate her supper with Jane while they planned and plotted ways and means of cutting down expenses.

It was ridiculous, thought Eulalia, that they had to go on living in this big house just because some ancestor had arranged matters to please himself. Her grandfather couldn't even let it to anyone; he must live in it until he died and pass it on to a nephew who lived on the other side of the world. The family solicitor had done his best but the law, however quaint, was the law. Trusts, however ancient, couldn't be overset unless one was prepared to spend a great deal of money and probably years of learned arguing...

Eulalia ate her supper, helped Jane tidy the kitchen and observed with satisfaction that tomorrow was Saturday.

'I'll get Grandfather into his chair and then do the shopping.'

She frowned as she spoke; pay day was still a week away and the housekeeping purse was almost empty. The Colonel's pension was just enough to pay for the maintenance of the house and Jane's wages; her own wages paid for food and what Jane called keeping up appearances.

What we need, reflected Eulalia, is a miracle.

And one was about to happen.

There was no sign of it in the morning, though. Jane was upstairs making the beds, the Colonel had been heaved from his bed and sat in his chair and Eulalia had loaded the washing machine and sat down to make a shopping list. Breast of chicken for the Colonel, macaroni cheese for Jane and herself, tea, sugar, butter... She was debating the merits of steak and kidney pudding over those of a casserole when the washing machine, long past its prime, came to a shuddering stop.

Usually it responded to a thump, even a sharp kick, but this morning it remained ominously silent. Extreme measures must be taken, decided Eulalia, and searched for a spanner—a useful tool she had discovered when there was no money for a plumber...

Mr van der Leurs, unaware that he was the miracle Eulalia wished for, paid off his taxi and made his way to the Colonel's house. A man esteemed by the members of his profession, renowned for his brilliant surgery, relentlessly pursued by ladies anxious to marry him, he had remained heart-whole, aware that somewhere on this earth there was the woman he would love and marry and until then he would bury his handsome nose in work. But his patience had been rewarded; one glimpse of Eulalia and he knew that he had found that woman. Now all he had to do was to marry her...

He reached the house and rang the bell and presently the door was opened and Eulalia stood there in a grubby pinny, looking cross. She still had the spanner in her hand, too. He saw that he would need to treat her with the same care with which he treated the more fractious of his small patients.

His 'Good morning' was briskly friendly. 'This is Colonel Langley's house? I wondered if I might visit him? My father was an old friend of his—van der Leurs.' He held out a hand. 'I am Aderik van der Leurs, his son.'

Eulalia offered a hand rather reluctantly. 'Grandfather has talked about a Professor van der Leurs he met years ago...'

Mr van der Leurs watched her face and read her thoughts accurately.

'I'm visiting at St Chad's for a few days,' he told her. 'Mr Curtis mentioned that the Colonel was housebound with arthritis and might be glad to have a visit. I have called at an awkward time, perhaps...'

He must be all right if Mr Curtis knew him, decided Eulalia.

'I think Grandfather would be pleased to see you. Come in; I'll take you to his room.'

She led him across the hall but before she reached the staircase she turned to look at him.

'I suppose you wouldn't know how to

make a washing machine start again?'

He had been wondering about the spanner. He said with just the right amount of doubt in his voice, 'Shall I take a look?'

She led him into the kitchen and Mr van der Leurs gave his full attention to the machine just as though it were one of his small patients on the operating table awaiting his skill. After a moment he took the spanner from her hand, tapped the dial very very gently and rotated it. The machine gave a gurgle and when he tapped it again—the mere whisper of a tap—it came to life with a heartening swish.

Eulalia heaved a sigh of relief. 'Thank you very much How clever of you, but I dare say you know something about washing machines.' She added doubtfully, 'But you're a doctor.'

He didn't correct her. 'I'm glad I could be of help,' he said, and then stood looking at her with a look of faint enquiry.

She said quickly, 'I'll take you to see Grandfather. He loves to have visitors.'

She took off her pinny and led the way into the hall and up the graceful staircase. It was a cold house—although there were radiators along the walls, none of them gave warmth. Outside the Colonel's door Eulalia stopped. 'I'll bring coffee up presently—you'll stay for that?'

'If I may.'

She knocked and opened the door and

then led him into the large room, pleasantly warm with a bright gas fire. There was a bed at one end of the room, bookshelves and a table by the wide window and several comfortable chairs. The Colonel sat in one of them, a reading lamp on the small table beside him, but he looked up as they went in. He eyed Mr van der Leurs for a moment. 'The spitting image of your father,' he observed. 'This is indeed a surprise—a delightful one, I might add.'

Mr van der Leurs crossed the room and gently shook the old hand with its swollen joints. 'A delight for me too, sir; Father talked of you a great deal.'

'Sit down if you can spare an hour. Lally, would you bring us coffee? You have met each other, of course?'

'Yes, Grandpa, I'll fetch the coffee.'

Mr van der Leurs watched her go out of the room. She wasn't only beautiful, he reflected, she was charming and her voice was quiet. He sat down near the Colonel, noting that the radiators under the window were giving off a generous warmth This room might be the epitome of warmth and comfort but that couldn't be said of the rest of the house.

Eulalia, going back to the kitchen, wondered about their visitor. He had said that he was at St Chad's. A new appointment? she wondered. Usually such news filtered down to the canteen sooner or later but she had heard nothing. In any case it was most unlikely that she would see him there. Consultants came to Outpatients, of course, but their consulting rooms were at the other end and they certainly never went near the canteen. Perhaps he was visiting to give lectures.

She ground the coffee beans they kept especially for her grandfather and got out the coffee pot and the china cups and saucers, and while she arranged them on a tray she thought about Mr van der Leurs.

He was a handsome man but not so very young, she decided. He had nice blue eyes and a slow smile which made him look younger than he was. He was a big man and tall but since she was a tall girl and splendidly built she found nothing unusual about that. Indeed, it was pleasant to look up to someone instead of trying to shrink her person.

She found the Bath Oliver biscuits and arranged them on a pretty little plate and bore the tray upstairs and found the two men in deep conversation. The Colonel was obviously enjoying his visitor and she beamed at him as she handed him his coffee and put the biscuits where her grandfather could reach them easily. She went away then, nursing a little glow of pleasure because Mr van der Leurs had got up when she had gone in and taken the tray and stayed on his feet until she had gone.

Nice manners, thought Eulalia as she went downstairs to have her coffee with Jane.

'I heard voices,' observed Jane, spooning instant coffee into mugs.

Eulalia explained. 'And Grandfather was pleased to see him.'

'He sounds all right. I remember his dad; came visiting years ago.'

'He got the washing machine to go again.'

'That's a mercy. Now, Miss Lally, you do your shopping; I'll hang out the washing— see if you can get a couple of those small lamb cutlets for the Colonel and a bit of steak for us—or mince. I'll make a casserole for us and a pie if there's enough...'

Eulalia got her coat from the hall and fetched a basket and sat down at the table to count the contents of her purse. A week to pay day so funds were low.

'It had better be mince,' she said. 'It's cheaper.' And then she added, 'I hate mince...'

She looked up and saw that Jane was smiling—not at her but at someone behind her. Mr van der Leurs was standing in the doorway holding the coffee tray.

'Delicious coffee,' he observed, 'and I was delighted to meet the Colonel.'

Eulalia got up and turned round to face him. 'Thank you for bringing down the tray. This is Jane, our housekeeper and friend.'

He crossed the room and shook hands with her and smiled his slow smile so that she lost her elderly heart to him.

'Miss Lally's just going to do the shopping,' she told him.

'Perhaps I may be allowed to carry the basket?'

And very much to her surprise Eulalia found herself walking out of the house with him and down a narrow side street where there was a row of small shops, old-fashioned and tucked discreetly behind the rather grand houses.

She asked, 'Don't you have to go back to the hospital? I mean, this is kind of you but you don't have to.'

'It's more or less on my way,' said Mr van der Leurs, and since she was too polite to ask where he was going and he had no intention of telling her she made polite small talk until they reached the shops.

The grocer's was small and rather dark but he sold everything. Mr van der Leurs, without appearing to do so, noted that she bought Earl Grey, the finest coffee beans, Bath Olivers, farm butter, Brie and Port Salut cheese, Cooper's marmalade and a few slices of the finest bacon; and, these bought, she added cheap tea bags, a tin of instant coffee, a butter substitute, sugar and flour and streaky bacon.

It was the same at the butcher's, where

she bought lamb cutlets, a chicken breast, lamb's kidneys and then minced beef and some sausages. He hadn't gone into the shop with her but had stood outside, apparently studying the contents of the window. At the greengrocer's he followed her in to take the basket while she bought potatoes and a cabbage, celery, carrots and a bunch of grapes.

'We make our own bread,' said Eulalia, bypassing the baker.

Mr van der Leurs, keeping his thoughts to himself, made light-hearted conversation as they returned to the house. It was evident to him that living was on two levels in the Colonel's house, which made it a sensible reason for him to marry her as quickly as possible. There were, of course, other reasons, but those, like his thoughts, he kept to himself.

At the house he didn't go in but as he handed over the basket he said, 'Will you have lunch with me tomorrow? We might drive out into the country. I find the weekends lonely.'

It was a good thing that his numerous friends in London hadn't heard him say that. He had sounded very matter-of-fact about it, which somehow made her feel sorry for him. A stranger in a foreign land, thought Eulalia, ignoring the absurd idea; he seemed perfectly at home in London and his English was as good as her own.

'Thank you, I should like that.'

'I'll call for you about eleven o'clock.' He smiled at her. 'Goodbye, Eulalia.'

Jane thought it was a splendid idea. 'Time you had a bit of fun,' she observed, 'and a good meal out somewhere posh.'

'It will probably be in a pub,' answered Eulalia.

She told her grandfather when she carried up his lunch.

'Splendid, my dear; he's a sound chap, just like his father was. I've asked him to come and see me again. He tells me he is frequently in England although he has his home in Holland.'

Eulalia, getting the tea later while Jane had a rest, spent an agreeable hour deciding what she would wear. It was nearing the end of October but the fine weather had held although it was crisply cold morning and evening. She decided on a short jacket, a pleated skirt and a silk jersey top, all of them old but because they had been expensive and well cut they presented an elegant whole. He had said that they would drive into the country, which might mean a pub lunch, but if it were to be somewhere grander she would pass muster...

When he called for her he was wearing beautifully cut tweeds, by no means new but bearing the hallmark of a master tailor, and his polished shoes were handmade. Even to an untutored eye he looked exactly what he was—a man of good taste and with the means to indulge it. Moreover, reflected Eulalia happily, her own outfit matched his.

He went to see her grandfather, to spend ten minutes with him and give him a book they had been discussing, and then stopped to talk to Jane, who was hovering in the hall, before he swept Eulalia out of the house and into the dark grey Bentley parked on the kerb.

'Is this yours?' asked Eulalia.

'Yes. I need to get around when I'm over here.' He glanced at her. 'Comfortable? Warm enough? It's a lovely morning but there's a nip in the air.'

He took the M4 out of London and turned off at Maidenhead. 'I thought the Cotswolds? We could lunch at Woodstock and drive on from there. A charming part of England, isn't it? You don't need to hurry back?'

'No. Jane likes to go to Evensong but I expect we shall be back long before then. Do you know this part of England well?'

'Not as well as I should like but each time I come here I explore a little more.'

He had turned off the A423 and was driving along country roads, through small villages and the quiet countryside to stop presently at North Stoke, a village by the Thames where they had coffee at a quiet pub. He talked quietly as he drove, undemanding, a placid flow of nothing much. By the time they reached

Woodstock, Eulalia was wishing the day would go on for ever.

The Feathers was warm and welcoming, with a pleasant bar and a charming restaurant. Eulalia, invited to choose her lunch, gulped at the prices and then, urged by her companion, decided on lobster patties and then a traditional Sunday lunch—roast beef, Yorkshire pudding, roast potatoes, vegetables...and after that a trifle to put to shame any other trifle. Eulalia finally sighed with repletion and poured the coffee.

'What a heavenly meal,' she observed. 'I shall remember it for years.'

'Good. The Cotswolds are at their best in the autumn, I think.'

He drove to Shipton-under-Wychwood, on to Stow-on-the-Wold and then Bourton-on-the-Water where he obligingly stopped for a while so that she might enjoy its charm and the little river running through the village. At Burford they stopped for tea at a hotel in its steep main street, a warm and cosy place where they sat in a pleasant room by the fire and ate toasted teacakes oozing butter and drank the finest Assam tea.

'This is bliss,' said Eulalia, mopping a buttery mouth. She smiled at him across the little table. 'I've had a heavenly day. Now we have to go back, don't we?'

'I'm afraid so. I'll settle up and see you at the car.'

Eulalia, powdering her beautiful nose, made a face at her reflection.

This has been a treat, she told herself. It isn't likely to happen again and so I mustn't like him too much. Even if I were to meet him at St Chad's it wouldn't be the same; he might not even recognise me. He'll go back to Holland and forget me.

It was already getting dusk and this time Mr van der Leurs took the main roads, travelling at a steady fast pace while they carried on an easy flow of small talk. But for all that, thought Eulalia as they were once more enclosed by the city's suburbs, she still knew almost nothing about him. Not that that mattered since she was unlikely to see him again. She hadn't asked him when he was going back to Holland but she supposed that it would be soon.

At the house, he came in with her. They were met by Jane in the hall.

'You'll have had your tea, but the kettle's boiling if you'd like another cup. The Colonel's nicely settled until supper time. I'm off to church.'

She smiled at them both. 'You've had a nice day?'

'Oh, Jane, it was heavenly.'

'I thought it might be. I'll get my hat and coat.'

'I don't suppose you want more tea?' Eulalia asked Aderik.

'I'd love a cup. While you are getting it may I have five minutes with the Colonel?'

'He'd like that. Do you want me to come up with you?'

'No, no. I know my way. I won't stay more than a few minutes.'

He went up the staircase, tapped on the Colonel's door and, bidden to enter, did so.

The Colonel was sitting in his chair doing a jigsaw puzzle but he pushed it to one side when Mr van der Leurs went in.

'Aderik. You had a pleasant day? Where did you go?'

Mr van der Leurs sat down beside him and gave him a succinct account of the day.

'You found Lally good company? She goes out so seldom. Never complains but it's no life for a girl. I do wonder what will happen to her when I am no longer here. She can't stay here—the place has to go to a nephew. A good chap but married with children.'

'Perhaps I can put your mind at rest about that, sir. I intend to marry Eulalia.'

The Colonel stared at him and then slowly smiled. 'Not wasted much time, have you?'

'I'm thirty-eight. Those years have been wasted romantically. I fell in love with her when I first saw her at St Chad's a day or two ago. I see no reason to waste any more time. You have no objection?'

'Good Lord, no. And your father would have liked her, as I'm sure your mother will.' He paused to think. 'She has no idea of your intentions?'

'None.'

'Well, I'm sure you know how you intend to go about that. You have lifted a load off my mind, Aderik. She's a dear girl and she has a loving heart.'

Mr van der Leurs got up and the Colonel offered a hand. 'You'll stay for supper?'

'No. I think not; enough is as good as a feast. Is that not so?'

The colonel rumbled with laughter. 'You're very like your father. Goodnight, my boy.'

Eulalia was in the kitchen. She and Jane were to have jacket potatoes for their supper but it was hardly a dish to offer to a guest. She hadn't asked him to stay to supper but she expected him to. She made the tea and when he entered the kitchen gave him a worried look.

'Shall we have tea here? Would you like to stay for supper?' She didn't sound at all eager and he hid a smile.

'Thank you but I mustn't stay. I've an appointment this evening. Tea would be fine.'

He drank his tea, waved aside her thanks for her day out, bade her a brisk goodbye and drove himself away. Eulalia shut the door as the Bentley slipped away, feeling hurt and a little peevish. He could at least have waved; it was almost as if he couldn't get away fast enough.

She poured herself another cup of tea. Of course he might be late for his appointment—with a girl? She allowed her imagination to run riot and then told herself sternly to stop being a fool. He was almost a stranger; she had only met him a couple of times; she knew nothing about him... So why was it that she felt so at ease with him, as though she had known him all her life?

> **DID YOU KNOW?**
> 'Xmas' is not a non-religious abbreviation of Christmas. It is derived from the Greek word for Christ—the first letter, 'chi', is the same as our letter 'x'.

If she had hoped to see him at the hospital the next day, she was disappointed. Her journeys into the hospital proper were limited to her visits to the supply department, the general office for requisitioning something for the canteen or taking money from the canteen at the end of the day to one of the clerical staff to lock away, but those trips took her nowhere near the wards and, since she had no idea as to what he actually did, even if she had the opportunity she had no idea where to look for him.

Filling rolls with cheese as the first of the day's patients began to surge in, she told herself to forget him.

Since it was the haematology outpatients clinic the benches were filling up fast. She recognised several of the patients as she poured tea and offered rolls. Anaemia in its many guises took a long time to cure, and if not to cure at least to check for as long as possible...

The clinic was due to start at any moment. She glanced towards the end of the waiting room to the row of consulting rooms and almost dropped the teapot she was filling. Mr van der Leurs, enormous in a white coat, was going into the first room, flanked by two young doctors and a nurse.

'But he's a mister,' said Eulalia to the teapot. 'A surgeon, so why is he at this clinic?' She had picked up quite a bit of knowledge since she had been working at St Chad's, not all of it accurate but she was sure that haematology was a medical field. He had disappeared, of course, and he wouldn't have seen her.

In this she was mistaken.

When the clinic was finally over she was at the back of the canteen getting ready for the afternoon's work and didn't see him leave.

It was six o'clock by the time she had closed the canteen, checked the takings and locked up. She put on her coat, picked up the bag of money and went through to the hospital. The clerk on night duty would lock it away and she would be free to go home. It was a pity that she had seen Mr van der Leurs again, she reflected. It had unsettled her.

She handed over the money and made for the main door. With any luck she wouldn't have to wait too long for a bus and the rush hour was over.

She pushed open the swing doors and walked full tilt into Mr van der Leurs.

He said easily, 'Ah, Eulalia, I was on my way to look for you. I have a book for your grandfather and I wondered if you would like a lift?'

She said slowly, 'I saw you in Outpatients this morning. I thought you were a surgeon—Mr, you know?'

He had taken her arm and was leading her to where the Bentley was parked.

'I am a surgeon, but I do a good deal of bone marrow transplanting and I had been asked to take a look at several patients who might benefit from that.'

He popped her into the car, got in beside her and drove away.

Eulalia said, 'Oh, I see,' which wasn't very adequate as a reply but it was all she could think of, and she answered his casual enquiry as to her day just as briefly; she hadn't expected to see him again and it had taken her by surprise.

He went straight up to the Colonel's room when they reached the house and when he came down again after ten minutes or so she was in the hall. There wasn't a fire in the drawing room. If he accepted her offer of coffee he would have to drink it in the kitchen; the drawing room would be icy...

He refused her offer. 'I'm leaving for Holland in the morning,' he told her, then he smiled down at her, shook her hand, and was gone.

PART TWO

JANE came to the kitchen door. 'Gone, has he? Well, it was shepherd's pie for supper; I doubt if he would have fancied that. I'll get a tin of salmon in the house; if he comes again, unexpected, like, I can make fishcakes.'

Eulalia said quietly, 'No need, Jane; he's going back to Holland in the morning.'

'You'll miss him...'

'I don't really know him, but yes, I shall miss him.'

Which was exactly what Mr van der Leurs had hoped for.

She was pouring tea for the thirsty queue towards the end of Thursday's afternoon clinic when she looked up and saw him. She put the teapot down with a thump and hoped that she didn't look as pleased as she felt; he had, after all, bidden her goodbye without a backward glance...

The queue parted for him to watch and listen with interest.

'I'll be outside the entrance,' he told her, smiled impartially at the queue and went

on his way.

''E was 'ere last week,' said a voice. 'Looking at my Jimmy—ever so nice 'e was, too.'

'A friend of yours, miss?' asked another voice.

'An acquaintance,' said Eulalia in a voice which forbade confidences of any sort, her colour somewhat heightened. The queue dissolved, the last few patients were called, she began to clear up, and presently, the hall empty, Sue and Polly gone, she closed down for the day.

The clerk kept her talking when she took the money to the office. He was an elderly man and night duty was a lonely job and she was too kind and polite to show impatience while he talked. Perhaps Mr van der Leurs would think that she didn't intend to meet him. She hadn't said that she would, had she? And if it had been a casual offer made on the spur of the moment, he might not wait.

He was there, leaning against the Bentley's bonnet, oblivious of the chilly evening. He opened the door for her as she reached him and got in beside her.

'Could we go somewhere for a cup of coffee? I haven't much time...'

'You can have coffee at home—' began Eulalia, and was cut short by his curt,

'There's a café in the Fulham Road; that

is the quickest way.'

She said tartly, 'If you are so pressed for time you had no need to give me a lift.'

He didn't answer but drove through the city. The café he ushered her into was small and half empty. He sat her down at a table away from the other customers, ordered coffee and observed in a matter-of-fact voice, 'This isn't quite what I intended but it will have to do. I got held up.'

The coffee came and Eulalia took a sip. 'I thought you were in Holland.'

'I was; I came over on the fast ferry this afternoon. I must go back on the ferry from Dover in a couple of hours' time.'

'You mean you're only here for an hour or two? Whatever for?'

'I wanted to see you and as I'm going to be away for a few days...'

'But you could have seen me at home or at the hospital.'

'Don't interrupt, Eulalia; there isn't time. It is enough to say that I wanted to see you alone.'

He smiled then and sat back, quite at his ease. 'Will you marry me, Eulalia?'

She opened her pretty mouth and closed it again and stared at him, sitting there asking her to marry him in a manner one would use to ask for the sugar.

'No,' said Eulalia.

He didn't look in the least put out. 'There are a dozen reasons why you should say no. Perhaps you will think about them while I'm away and when I see you again we can discuss them.' He smiled at her. 'I shall see you again, you know, and next time we can talk at our leisure. Now I'm afraid I must take you home.'

Eulalia could think of nothing to say; she tried out several sensible remarks to make in her head but didn't utter them. She could, of course, tell him that she didn't want to see him again but somehow she didn't say so. Later she would think of all kinds of clever replies to make but he wouldn't be there to hear them. And she mustn't see him again.

He drove the short distance to the Colonel's house, got out and went with her to the door.

'Well, goodbye,' said Eulalia, and offered a hand.

'Not goodbye; we say *tot ziens*.' He shook her hand briefly and opened the door for her.

As he turned away she asked, 'Where are you going?'

'Albania.'

'But that's... Oh, do take care!'

He stood looking down at her for a moment, his eyes half hidden under their heavy lids. Just for a moment Eulalia had let her heart speak for itself.

Driving down to Dover and once on the

other side of the Channel, taking the long road home, Mr van der Leurs allowed his thoughts to dwell on a pleasant future.

October became November and brought cold wind and rain and grey skies, none of which lightened Eulalia's mood. Mr van der Leurs had been gone for a week and she worried about him, and although she told herself that he was old enough and large enough to take care of himself she scanned the papers and listened to the news and wished that there was some way of finding out if he was back home...

The Colonel, expressing a wish to see him again, had to be told.

'He'll be back. Miss him, do you, Lally?'

Arranging his bedside table just so for the night, she admitted that she did, kissed him fondly and bade him sleep well.

The Colonel, waiting for sleep, thought contentedly that he had no need to worry about Lally's future; Aderik would take care of it. He drifted off gently and died peacefully as he slept.

Somehow or other Eulalia got through the next few days. There was a great deal to do—not least the nephew to notify. There were no other family but old friends had to be told, notices printed in *The Times* and *Telegraph*, the bank manager, his solicitor informed, arrangements for the funeral made. The nephew arrived after two days, a middle-aged kindly man who needed to be housed and fed.

There was no question of Eulalia leaving the house until she had made her own arrangements, he told her. He had a wife and four children who would be coming to England shortly but the house was large enough—he had no intention of turning her out of her home. She thanked him, liking him for his concern, and listened politely to his plans. He was an artist of some repute and was delighted to return to London; the house was large enough to house his family in comfort, and there were attics which could be turned into a studio.

His wife and children arrived in time for the funeral so that Eulalia, opening rooms again, getting ready for their arrival, had little time to grieve. After the funeral he would return to sort out his affairs but his wife and children would remain.

Tom and Pam couldn't have been kinder to her, and the children, although circumstances had subdued them, brought the house alive. Somehow, the funeral which she had been dreading turned into a dignified and serene occasion, with the Colonel's old friends gathered there, making themselves known to Tom and Pam, shaking Eulalia by the hand, asking about her job, telling her in their elderly voices that she was a pretty girl and wasn't it time she married.

However, there were still the nights to get through; there was time to grieve then and wonder what the future held for her.

She would have to leave the house, of course, despite Pam's kind insistence that she could stay as long as she wanted to. But at least Jane's future was safe; she was to remain as housekeeper.

The Colonel had left Eulalia his small capital—enough to supplement her wages so that she could rent somewhere. But London was expensive; she would have to find somewhere nearer the hospital and even then she would be eating into her bank balance with little chance of saving. Perhaps she should move away from London, find a job in a small town where she could live cheaply...

She was on compassionate leave from her work but she continued to get up early to go down to the kitchen and help Jane. Still in her dressing gown, her hair hanging tangled down her back, she made tea for them both, laid the breakfast table, fed the cat and cut the bread while Jane made porridge and collected bacon, eggs and mushrooms.

The new owners of the house enjoyed a good breakfast and Jane, now that she had a generous housekeeping allowance, was happy to cook for hearty eaters. After the skimping and saving she and Eulalia had lived with, it was a treat to use her cooking skills once more. And her future was secure. The one thing which troubled her was Miss Lally, brushing aside her worried questions as to where she was to go and how she would manage, assuring her that she would have no trouble in finding a nice little flat and making lots of friends.

She looked across at Eulalia now, a worried frown on her elderly face. She was beautiful even in that elderly dressing gown with her hair anyhow, but she was pale and too thin. She said, 'Miss Lally...' and was interrupted by the front door knocker being thumped.

'Postman's early,' said Eulalia, and went to open it.

Mr van der Leurs stood there, looking larger than ever in the dim light of the porch lamp.

Eulalia stared up at him, burst into tears and flung herself into his arms. He held her close while she sobbed and snuffled into his cashmere overcoat, unheeding of the early morning wind whistling around them. But when she had no more tears, sucking in her breath like a child, he swept her into the house, shut the door and offered her his handkerchief, still with one arm around her.

'Grandfather died,' said Eulalia into his shoulders. 'I'm sorry I've cried all over you but, you see, I didn't know it was you and I was so glad...'

A muddled speech which Mr van der Leurs received with some satisfaction. 'Tell me about it, Eulalia.' He propelled her gently into the kitchen, nodded pleasantly to an astonished Jane and sat Eulalia down at the table.

'You don't object to me coming into your kitchen? Eulalia is rather upset. If I might just stay and hear what has happened...'

'It's a blessing that you've come, sir.' Jane was already pouring boiling water into a teapot. 'You just sit there for as long as you like and don't mind me.'

So he pulled out a chair and sat down beside Eulalia. Nothing would ever dim her beauty, he reflected: tousled hair, pink nose, childish sniffs and wrapped in a garment which he supposed was a dressing gown, cut apparently with a knife and fork out of a sack. He asked quietly, 'When did the Colonel die, Eulalia?'

She gave a final sniff and sipped some tea and told him. Her voice was watery but she didn't cry again and he didn't interrupt her. Only when she had finished he said gently, 'Go and get dressed, Eulalia. Tell Tom that you are going out to have breakfast with me and will be back later.'

When she hesitated he added, 'I'm sure Jane thinks that is a good idea.'

Jane said at once, 'Just what she needs—to get away from us all for a bit, talk about it, make a few plans.'

She gave Mr van der Leurs a sharp look and he smiled. 'Just so, Jane!'

Lally went to the door. She turned round when she reached it. 'You won't go away?'

He got up and opened the door for her. 'No, I won't go away, but don't be long; I'm hungry.'

A remark which made everything seem perfectly normal. Just as it seemed perfectly normal to find the Bentley outside. It was only as they were driving through the early morning traffic that Eulalia asked, 'How long have you been back?'

'I got to Schiphol late last night, went home and got the car and took the late night ferry from Ostend.'

'But you haven't been to bed. You haven't got to go to St Chad's and work...?'

'No. No, I wanted to see you.'

She said faintly, 'But don't you want to get some sleep?'

'Yes, but there are several things I want to do first. We'll go to Brown's and have breakfast.'

It seemed that he was known there. The doorman welcomed them with a cheerful 'Good morning', summoned up someone to park the car and held the door open for them. It was quiet, pleasantly warm inside and for the moment free of people. They sat at a table by a window and an elderly waiter assured them that the porridge was excellent and did they fancy kedgeree?

It wasn't until they were eating toast and marmalade and another pot of coffee had been brought that Mr van der Leurs made any attempt at serious conversation. Only when she asked him how long he would be in London did he tell her that he would be returning to Holland that evening.

When she protested, 'But you can't—you've not been to bed; you must be tired,' he only smiled.

One or two people had come to eat their breakfasts, exchanging polite 'Good mornings' and opening their newspapers. Eulalia leaned across the table, anxious not to be heard.

'Why have you brought me here?'

'To eat breakfast,' he said promptly, and smiled when she said crossly,

'You know that isn't what I mean.'

He said, suddenly serious, 'You know that if I had known about the Colonel I would have come at once?'

'Yes. I don't know quite how I know that, but I do.'

'Good. Eulalia, will you marry me?'

'You asked me once already...'

'In somewhat different circumstances. Your grandfather knew of my intentions and thought it was a good idea.'

She stared at him. 'After I told you I wouldn't...'

'Yes.'

'You mean you were going to ask me again?'

'Of course.' He sounded matter-of-fact.

'Shall we go for a walk and talk about it?'

When she nodded, he added, 'I'll book a table for lunch here. I'll drive you back on my way to the ferry afterwards.'

It was as if he had lifted all her worries and doubts onto his own shoulders, she reflected.

They walked to Hyde Park. There were few people there: dog owners and joggers and a few hardy souls who had braved the chilly November morning. Mr van der Leurs hardly spoke and Eulalia, busy with her chaotic thoughts, hardly noticed. They had walked the length of the Serpentine before he said, 'It is high time that I married, Eulalia, but until I met you I hadn't given it much thought. I need a wife—a professional man does—but I want a friend and a companion too, someone sensible enough to see to my home, to be a hostess to my friends, and cope with the social side of my life. You know nothing of me but if we marry you may have all the time you wish for to get to know me.'

Eulalia said gravely, 'But doesn't love come into it?'

'Later, and only if you wish it...'

'You mean you would be quite happy to have me as—as a friend until I'd got used to you?'

He hid a smile. 'Very neatly put, Eulalia; that is just what I mean. And now let us look at the practical side. You have no home, no money and no prospects, whereas I can offer you a home, companionship and a new life.'

He stopped walking and turned her round to face him. 'I promise you that I will make you happy.'

She looked up into his face. 'I believe you,' she told him, 'but have you considered that you might meet a woman you could fall in love with?'

'Yes, I have thought about that too. I am thirty-eight, my dear; I have had ample time in which to fall in love a dozen times—and out again.'

'I've never been in love,' she told him. 'Oh, I had teenage crushes on film stars and tennis players but I never met any young men once I'd left school and gone to live with Grandfather. I know almost everyone at St Chad's. But I'm just the canteen lady; besides, I'm twenty-seven.'

Mr van der Leurs restrained himself from gathering her into his arms and hugging her. Instead he said, 'It is obvious to me that we are well suited to each other.'

He took her arm and walked on. Since he was obviously waiting for her to say something, Eulalia said, 'You asked me to marry you. I will.'

And she added, 'And if it doesn't work out you must tell me...'

He stopped once more and this time took her in his arms and kissed her gently, a very light, brief kiss. He said, 'Thank you, Eulalia.'

They walked on again with her arm tucked under his. Presently he said, 'I shall be away for several days after which I can arrange for a day or so to be free. Would you consider marrying by special licence then? I know it is all being arranged in a rush and in other circumstances I wouldn't have suggested it. But I can see no good reason for you to remain any longer than you must at Tom's house. I'm sure he would never suggest that you should leave before you are ready but you can't be feeling too comfortable about it.'

'Well, no, I'm not. Tom is very kind and so is Pam but I'm sure they'll be glad to see me go. I shall miss Jane...'

'Is she also leaving? She may come with you, if you wish.'

'Tom has asked her to stay as housekeeper and she has agreed. She's lived there for years.'

They were retracing their steps. She glanced up at him and saw how tired he was. She said warmly, 'I'll be ready for whatever day you want us to marry. Must I do anything?'

'No... I'll see to everything. If you would give me the name of your local clergyman and his church, as soon as everything is settled I'll let you know.' He added, 'It will be a very quiet wedding, no bridesmaids and wedding gown, no guests...'

'I wouldn't want that anyway. It would be a sham, wouldn't it? What I mean is we're marrying for...' She sought for words. 'We're not marrying for the usual reasons, are we?'

He reflected that his reasons were the same as any man in love but he could hardly say so. He said merely, 'I believe that we shall be happy together. And now let us go back and have our lunch...'

They had the same table and the same waiter—a dignified man who permitted himself a smile when Mr van der Leurs ordered champagne.

'The lobster Thermidor is to be recommended,' he suggested.

So they ate lobster and drank champagne and talked about this and that—rather like a married couple who were so comfortable in each other's company that there was no need to say much. Eulalia, spooning Charlotte Russe, felt as though she had known Aderik all her life, which was exactly what he had intended her to think. She liked him and she trusted him and in time she would love him but he would have to have patience...

He drove her back to the house presently and spent ten minutes talking to Tom before leaving. He bade Eulalia goodbye without wasting time and drove away, leaving her feeling lonely and all of a sudden uncertain.

'What you need,' said Pam, 'is a cup of tea. We're delighted for you—Tom and I would never have turned you out, you know, but you're young and have your own life and he seems a very nice man. I'm sure you'll be happy. What shall you wear?'

'Wear?'

'For the wedding, of course.'

'I haven't any clothes – I mean, nothing new and suitable.'

'Well, I don't suppose you'll need to buy much; your Aderik looks as though he could afford to keep a wife. Tom told me that his uncle has left you a little money. Spend it, dear; he would have wanted you to be a beautiful bride.'

'But it'll be just us...'

'So something simple that you can travel in and wear later on. You go shopping tomorrow; he might be back sooner than you think and you must be ready.'

So the next morning Eulalia went to the bank and, armed with a well-filled purse, went shopping. It wasn't just something in which to be married that she needed; she was woefully short of everything. She went back at the end of the day, laden with plastic bags, and there were still several things which she must have. But she was satisfied with her purchases: a wool coat with a matching crêpe dress in grey and a little hat in velvet to go with them, a jersey dress, and pleated skirt and woolly jumpers and silk blouses, sensible shoes and a pair of high-heeled court shoes to go with the wedding outfit.

Tomorrow she would get a dressing gown and undies from Marks & Spencer. The question of something pretty to wear in case Aderik took her out for an evening was a vexatious one. She had spent a lot of money and there wasn't a great deal left, not sufficient to buy the kind of dress she thought he might like—plain and elegant and a perfect fit. She had seen such a dress but if she bought it it would leave her almost penniless and she had no intention of asking Aderik for money the moment they were married.

This was a tricky problem which was fortunately solved for her. Tom and Pam gave her a cheque for a wedding present, explaining that they had no idea what to give her. 'I'm sure Mr van der Leurs has everything he could possibly want, so spend it on yourself, Lally.'

It was a handsome sum, more than enough to buy the dress, and what was left over she could spend on something for Aderik and tell him it was from Tom and Pam.

Trying the dress on, Eulalia smiled at her reflection in the long mirror. It was exactly right; the colour of old rose, silk crêpe, its simple lines clinging to her splendid shape in all the right places. Perhaps she would

never wear it; she had no idea if Aderik had a social life but it would be there, hanging in her wardrobe, just in case...

She displayed it to Tom, Pam and Jane, and packed it away in the big leather suitcase which had belonged to her grandfather. She was quite ready now. Aderik hadn't phoned or written but she hadn't expected him to do so. He was a busy man; he had said that he would let her know when he was coming and it never entered her head to doubt him.

He phoned that evening, matter-of-fact and casual. He would be with her in two days' time and they were to marry on the following morning and travel back to Holland that evening. 'You are well?' he wanted to know. 'No problems?'

'No, none, and I'm quite ready. The Reverend Mr Willis phoned to say he was coming to see me this evening. I don't know why.'

'I asked him to. I don't want you to have any doubts, Eulalia!'

'Well, I haven't, but it will be nice to talk to him. I've known him a long time.'

'I'll see you shortly. I'm not sure what time I'll get to London.'

'I'll be waiting. You're busy? I won't keep you. Goodbye, Aderik.'

She could have wished his goodbye to have been a little less brisk...

Mr Willis came that evening; they had known each other for a number of years and it pleased her that he was going to marry them. 'I would have liked to have met your future husband before the wedding, Lally, but in the circumstances I quite understand that it is not possible. We had a long talk over the phone and I must say I was impressed. You are quite sure, aren't you? He has no doubts but perhaps you have had second thoughts?'

'Me? No, Mr Willis. I think we shall be happy together. Grandfather liked him, you know. And so do I...'

'He will be coming the day after tomorrow? And I understand you will be returning to Holland on the day of the wedding?'

'Yes, it all seems rather a scramble, doesn't it? But he has commitments at the hospital which he must keep and if we don't marry now, in the next day or so, he wouldn't be free for some time. Tom and his wife have been very kind to me but you can understand that I don't want to trespass on their hospitality for longer than I must.'

'Quite so. Both you and Mr van der Leurs are old enough not to do anything impetuous.'

Eulalia agreed, reflecting that buying the rose-pink dress had been impetuous. She didn't think that Mr van der Leurs had ever been impetuous; he would think seriously about something and once he had decided about it he would carry out whatever it was in a calm and unhurried manner...

Mr Willis went away presently after a little talk with Tom, and Eulalia went upstairs and tried on the pink dress once more...

Mr van der Leurs arrived just before midnight. Tom and Pam had become worried when he didn't arrive during the day but Eulalia was undisturbed. 'He said he would be here today, so he'll come. It may be late, though. You won't mind if I stay up and see him? We shan't have time to talk in the morning.'

So she sat in the kitchen with Dickens for company and everyone else went to bed. She had the kettle singing on the Aga and the coffee pot keeping warm. If he was hungry she could make sandwiches or make him an omelette. The house was very quiet and she had curled up in one of the shabby armchairs, allowing her thoughts to wander.

She had lived with the Colonel ever since she had been orphaned, gone to school, lived a quiet life, had friends, gone out and about until her grandfather had lost most of his money. It had been tied up in a foreign bank which had gone bankrupt. He had then been stricken with arthritis of such a crippling nature that there was little to be done for him. It was then that she had found a job. She supposed that if Aderik hadn't wanted to marry her she would have stayed there for the rest of her working life, living in a bedsitter, unwilling to accept Tom's offer of help.

'I'll be a good wife. It will be all right once I know more about him. And we like each other.' She addressed Dickens, sitting in his basket, and he stared at her before closing his eyes and going to sleep again.

He opened them again at the gentle knock on the door and Eulalia went to open it.

Mr van der Leurs came in quietly, dropped a light kiss on her cheek and put down his bag and his overcoat. 'I've kept you from your bed, but I couldn't get away earlier.'

'I wasn't sleepy. Would you like a meal? Come into the kitchen.'

'Coffee would be fine. I won't stay; I just wanted to make sure that everything was all right.'

She was warming milk. 'Have you got somewhere to stay?'

'Brown's. I'll be at the church at eleven o'clock. I've booked a table at Brown's for all of us afterwards. I arranged that with Tom. We can collect your luggage from here later and be in plenty of time for the evening ferry.'

'And when we get to Holland will you be able to have a few days' holiday?'

'A couple of days. You won't see a great deal of me, Eulalia, but as soon as it's possible I'll rearrange my work so that I can be home more often.'

They sat opposite each other at the table, not saying much. She could see that he was tired and she was pleasantly sleepy. Presently he got up, put their mugs tidily in the sink and went with her to the door, put on his coat and picked up his bag. Then he stood for a minute, looking down at her.

He had no doubts about his feelings for her; he had fallen in love with her and he would love her for ever. Now all he needed was patience until she felt the same way.

He bent and kissed her, slowly and gently this time. 'Sleep well, my dear.'

She closed the door behind him and went up to her room and ten minutes later was asleep, her last thoughts happy ones.

She was wakened by Jane with a breakfast tray.

'Brides always have breakfast in bed, Miss Lally, and Mrs Langley says you are to eat everything and no one will disturb you until you're dressed and ready.'

So Eulalia ate her breakfast and then, since it was her wedding day, took great pains with her hair and her face before getting into the dress and coat, relieved to see that they looked just as nice as they had done when she had bought them. And finally, with the little hat crowning her head, she went downstairs.

They were all there, waiting for her, ready to admire her and wish her well, and presently Pam and Jane and the children drove off to the church, leaving Eulalia and Tom to wait until it was time for him to get his own car from the garage and usher her into the back seat.

'Why can't I sit in the front with you?' asked Eulalia.

'Brides always sit in the back, Lally...'

The church was dimly lit, small and ancient and there were flowers. That much she noticed as they reached the porch. She clutched the little bouquet of roses which Aderik had sent that morning and took Tom's arm as they walked down the aisle to where she could see Mr Willis and Aderik's broad back. There was another man there too. The best man, of course. She dismissed him as unimportant and kept her eyes on Aderik. If only he would turn round...

He did, and gave her a warm, encouraging smile which made everything perfectly all right, and since there was nothing of the pomp and ceremony of a traditional wedding to distract her thoughts she listened to every word Mr Willis said and found them reassuring and somehow comforting. She wondered if Aderik was listening too and peeped up into his face. It was calm and thoughtful, and, reassured,

she held out her left hand so that he could slip the ring on her finger.

Leaving the church with him, getting into the Bentley with him, she touched the ring with a careful finger, remembering the words of the marriage service. She had made promises which she must keep...

Mr van der Leurs glanced at her serious face. 'The advantage of a quiet wedding is that one really listens, don't you agree?'

'Yes. I—I liked it.'

'And you looked delightful; I am only sorry that we have to hurry away so quickly. You still have to meet my best man—an old friend, Jules der Huizma. We see a good deal of each other. He's married to an English girl—Daisy—you'll meet her later and I hope you'll be friends.'

'Do they live near you? I'm not sure where you do live...'

'Amsterdam, but I was born in Friesland and my home is there. When I can arrange some free time I'll take you there to meet my family.'

'It's silly really, isn't it? I mean, we're married and I don't know anything about you.'

'True, but you know me, don't you, Eulalia? And that's important.'

She nodded. 'I feel as if I've known you for a very long time—you know? Like very old friends who don't often meet but know how the other one is feeling.'

Mr van der Leurs knew then that he had his heart's desire, or most of it. Perhaps he wouldn't have to wait too long before Eulalia fell in love with him. He would leave no stone unturned to achieve that.

The luncheon party at Brown's hotel was all that a wedding breakfast should be— champagne, lobster patties, chicken à la king, sea bass, salads, red onion tartlets, garlic mushrooms in a cream sauce and then caramelised fruits and ice cream and finally the wedding cake. When it was cut and Eulalia and Aderik's health had been drunk, he made a speech, gave brief thanks and offered regret that they couldn't stay longer and enjoy their friends' company. Then the best man, wishing them well, said he was delighted that he would see more of them in the future.

He seemed nice, thought Eulalia, and wondered why his Daisy wasn't with him— she must remember to ask…

Then it was time to go. She was kissed and hugged and Jane cried a little for they had been through some difficult years together. 'But I'll be back to see you,' said Eulalia. 'Aderik is often over here and I shall come with him.'

She turned and waved to the little group as they drove away. She was leaving a life she knew for an unknown future.

PART THREE

THEY travelled over to Holland on the catamaran from Harwich and were driving through the outskirts of Amsterdam before midnight. The crossing had been choppy and Eulalia was glad to be on dry land again. The lights of the city were welcoming and she felt a surge of excitement. They hadn't talked much, though Aderik had pointed out the towns they bypassed, but there was no way of seeing them in the dark night.

They had talked about the wedding and he had promised that he would show her as much as possible of Amsterdam before he went back to his usual working day. Now he said, 'I live in the centre of the city; we're coming to a main street— Overtoom—which leads to one of the main squares—Leidseplein—and a little further on I'll turn right onto the Herengracht; that's one of the canals which circle the old part of the city. The house is in a quiet street just off the canal and has been in my family for many years.'

There was plenty to see now. The streets were still bustling with people, cafés were brightly lighted, there were trams and buses and cars. Mr van der Leurs turned into a street running beside a canal bordered by trees and lined with tall narrow houses with steep gables and important-looking front doors.

Eulalia, wide awake by now despite the

lateness of the hour, said happily, 'Oh, it's like a painting by Pieter de Hooch...'

'True enough, since they might have been painted by him. They knew how to build in those days; all these houses are lived in still.'

He crossed a bridge and turned into a narrow street beside another, smaller canal also lined with trees and a row of gabled houses. The street was short and there was another bridge at its end, too small for cars, spanning yet another canal. It was very quiet, away from the main streets with only the bare trees stirring in the night wind, and as he stopped before the last house Eulalia asked, 'Is this where you live?'

'Yes. Are you very tired? I think that Ko and Katje will be waiting up for us.'

She assured him that she was wide awake as he opened her door and they crossed the street to his front door—a handsome one with an ornate transom above it—and it was now flung open wide as they mounted the two steps from the pavement.

Eulalia hadn't known what to expect. Aderik had scarcely mentioned his home,

and she had supposed that it would be a solid, comfortable house, the kind of house she imagined a successful man might live in. But this was something different. She was ushered in and the door was shut behind them before Mr van der Leurs spoke, and that in his own language to the stout, middle-aged man who had admitted them. Then he took her arm. 'Eulalia, this is Ko, who runs our home with his wife. Come and meet everyone.'

She shook hands with Ko who welcomed her in English and then shook hands with his wife, Katje, as stout as her husband, beaming good wishes which Aderik translated. Then there was Mekke, young and buxom, adding her good wishes in hesitant English, and lastly Wim, a small, wizened man 'who has been in the family for as long as I can remember', said Mr van der Leurs. 'He drives the car when I'm not around and sees to the garden.' He looked around him. 'Where is Humbert?'

They had taken the precaution, explained Ko, of putting him in the garden in case *mevrouw* was nervous of dogs.

Aderik looked at her. 'Are you nervous of dogs, Eulalia?'

'No, I like them. May he not come in and meet me? He must be wanting to see you again.'

Ko had understood her and trotted off through a door at the back of the hall.

'*Koffie?*' asked Katje, and trotted after

him, taking Mekke and Wim with her.

Mr van der Leurs turned Eulalia round, unbuttoned her coat and cast it on one of the splendid chairs flanking a console table worthy of a museum.

'Then come and meet Humbert.'

He opened a door and led her into a high-ceilinged room with an ornate plaster ceiling, tall narrow windows and a wide fireplace with a great hood above it. There was a splendid fire burning in the fire basket below, adding its light to the sconces on the walls hung with crimson silk. It was a magnificent room and Eulalia stood in the doorway and gaped at it.

But she wasn't allowed to stand and stare. 'This way,' said Aderik, and crossed the floor to another door at the end of the room, opposite the windows. This led to a little railed gallery with steps down to another room. A library, she supposed, for its walls were lined with shelves filled with books and there were small tables and comfortable chairs. But she had no chance to do more than look around her; the room led into a conservatory with a profusion of greenery and elegant cane furniture, and that opened onto the garden, which was narrow and high-walled and surprisingly large.

The dog that rushed to meet them was large too, a great shaggy beast who gave a delighted bark and hurled himself at his master. Then, at a word from Aderik the dog offered a woolly head for her to

scratch. Mr van der Leurs switched off the outside lights and closed the door to the garden, then led the way back to the library, through another door in the further wall. Here there was a veritable warren of small rooms until he finally opened the last door which brought them back into the hall.

'Tomorrow,' he assured her, 'you will be given a leisurely tour of the house. You must be tired; come and have a drink and something to eat and Katje will take you to your room.'

The *Stoelklok* in the hall chimed the hour as they went back into the drawing room where, on a small table by the fire, Ko was arranging a tray of coffee and a plate of sandwiches. Eulalia, half asleep now but excited too, drank her coffee, and, suddenly discovering that she was hungry, ate several sandwiches.

'What time do you have breakfast?'

'Since I am free tomorrow and we have all day before us, would half past eight suit you?'

She nodded. 'What time do you usually breakfast?'

'Half past seven. I walk to the hospital. If I have a list it starts at half past eight. If you would rather have your breakfast in bed that can easily be arranged.'

'I've only ever had breakfast in bed this morning and I like getting up early...'

'Splendid.' He got up and tugged the

bell-pull by the fireplace and when Katje came said, 'Sleep well, my dear. I'll see you at breakfast.'

Eulalia got up, longing now for her bed. She lifted her face for his kiss, quick and light on her cheek, and followed Katje up the oak staircase to the landing above. It was ringed by several doors and another staircase but Katje led her to the front of the house and opened a door with something of a flourish.

The room was already lit and heavy brocade curtains were drawn across the windows. There was a pale carpet underfoot and a Georgian mahogany and satinwood four-poster flanked by mahogany bedside tables faced the windows between which was a satinwood table with a triple mirror. There was a tapestry-covered stool before it and there were two Georgian armchairs on either side of a mahogany tallboy.

Eulalia caught her breath at the room's beauty as Katje bustled past her and opened the door in a wall, revealing a vast closet; she could see her few clothes hanging forlornly there; someone had unpacked already. Another door led to a bathroom, which Katje crossed to open yet another door, revealing a second room, handsomely furnished but simple.

Katje trotted back, smiling and nodding, and went away. Eulalia lost no time in undressing and bathing before tumbling into bed. The splendid room must be explored thoroughly but not tonight. She was asleep as her head touched the pillow.

She woke as Mekke was drawing back the curtains; the girl wished her a good morning and put a tea tray beside her. She said in English, 'Breakfast soon, *mevrouw*,' and went away. There was an ornate green enamel and gilt clock on the tallboy striking eight o'clock as she drank her tea.

Eulalia nipped from her bed and dressed quickly in a skirt, blouse and sweater, wasted time hanging out of the window in the cold morning air to view the quiet street outside and the canal beyond, then hurried downstairs. The house was alive with cheerful, distant voices and Humbert's deep bark as she reached the hall, uncertain where to go.

Aderik opened a door and then crossed the hall to her, kissed her cheek and wished her a good morning. 'You slept well? Come and have breakfast.'

He ushered her into a small room, very cosy with a small table laid ready for them, and Humbert came prancing to have his head scratched and grin at her.

Eulalia found her voice. 'What a dear little room. Did I see it last night?'

'We came through it but I doubt whether you saw it; you were asleep on your feet, weren't you?'

He smiled at her and pulled out a chair for her before sitting down himself. 'There's tea or coffee; you must let Ko know which you prefer to have.' He added kindly, 'It's all strange, isn't it? But you'll soon find your feet.'

Eulalia said slowly, 'I have the feeling that I shall wake up presently and find that none of this is happening.'

She buttered toast. 'It all happened so quickly...'

'Indeed it did, but now you can have all the time you want to adjust—it is merely that you will be doing it after we are married and not before. I imagine that you would have given your future a good deal of thought if we had waited to marry. You may still do so, Eulalia, and I hope that if you have doubts or problems you will tell me.'

'Yes, I will but I shan't bother you more than I must for you must be very occupied. What else do you do besides operating?'

'I have an outpatients clinic once a week, ward rounds, private patients at my consulting rooms, consultations—and from time to time I go over to St Chad's and occasionally to France or Germany.'

He saw the look on her face. 'But I am almost always free at the weekends and during the week there is the odd hour...'

Waiting for Eulalia in the hall presently, he watched her coming down the stairs. She was wearing a short jacket and no hat; a visit to a dress shop would have to be contrived; a warm winter coat was badly needed and some kind of a hat. It was

obvious to him that his dearest Lally was sorely in need of a new wardrobe. He said nothing; he was a man who had learned when to keep silent. In answer to her anxious enquiry he merely assured her that Humbert had had a long walk before breakfast.

'We will come home for lunch and take him for a walk in one of the parks,' he suggested. 'But now I'll show you something of Amsterdam.'

Mr van der Leurs loved his Amsterdam; his roots went deep for a long-ago ancestor had made a fortune in the Indies—a fortune which his descendants had prudently increased—and built himself the patrician house in the heart of the city. The house in which he had been born and grown to manhood. He had left it for long periods—medical school at Leiden, years at Cambridge, a period at Heidelberg—but now he was firmly established in his profession, making a name for himself, working as a consultant at St Chad's, travelling from time to time to other countries to lecture or examine or attend a consultation.

He wanted Eulalia to love Amsterdam too and, unlike the tours arranged for sightseers, he walked her through the narrow streets away from the usual sights. He showed her hidden canals away from the main *grachten*, old almshouses, houses built out beside the canals so that their back walls hung over the water. He showed her churches, a street market, the flower barges loaded down with colour, gave her coffee in a crowded café where men were playing billiards and the tables were covered with red and white checked cloths, and then wove his way into the elegant streets where the small expensive dress shops were to be found.

Before one of those plate-glass windows he paused.

'The coat draped over that chair...it would suit you admirably and you will need a thick topcoat; it can be so cold here in the winter. Shall we go inside and see if you like it?'

He didn't wait for her to answer but opened the door. Five minutes later Eulalia and he returned to the pavement and this time she was wearing the coat. It was navy blue cashmere and a perfect fit, while on her head was a rakish little beret. The jacket, the friendly saleslady had promised, would be sent to the house.

Eulalia stood in the middle of the pavement, regardless of passers-by. 'Thank you, Aderik,' she said. 'It's the most beautiful thing I've ever possessed.' Her eyes searched his quiet face. 'I—I haven't many clothes and they're not very new.' She looked away for a moment and then gave him a very direct look. 'I hope you're not ashamed of me?'

Mr van der Leurs realised the danger ahead. He said in a matter-of-fact voice, 'You look elegant in anything you wear, my dear, and you are beautiful enough to wear a sack and still draw interested glances. And no, I am not ashamed of you, but I don't want you catching cold when all that are needed are warmer clothes.'

He took her arm and walked on. 'I think that you must get a few things before winter really sets in.'

Put like that, it seemed a sensible suggestion. He glanced down at her face and saw with satisfaction the look of delighted anticipation on it.

They went back to a main street and caught a tram. It was in two sections and both of them were packed. Eulalia stood with his arm around her, loving every minute of it, and then scrambled off when they reached the point where the street intersected the Herengracht. They walked back home from there so that she could find her way back on her own.

They lunched in the small room where they had breakfasted with Humbert sitting between them, happy now that they were home, knowing that presently he would be taken for a walk.

They went to Vondel Park, a long walk which took them past the Rijksmuseum and through a tangle of small streets to the park. Here Humbert raced to and fro while they walked the paths briskly in the teeth of a cold wind.

'Tomorrow we will take the car,' said Mr van der Leurs cheerfully, 'so that you may get a glimpse of Holland. This is not the time of year to see it, of course, but the roads will be empty and we can cover a good deal of ground. You know of St Nikolaas, of course? You must see him with Zwarte Piet riding through the streets. It was once a great day but now we celebrate Christmas much as you do in England. All the same, we exchange small presents and the children have parties.'

He turned her round smartly and started the walk back to the park's gates. 'And after St Nikolaas there will be parties and concerts and the hospital ball and the family coming for Christmas.'

'The family?' asked Eulalia faintly. 'You have a large family?'

'Mother, brother and sisters, nieces and nephews, scattered around the country.'

'You didn't tell me. Do they know you have married me?'

'Yes, and they are delighted. I should have mentioned it; it quite slipped my mind.'

She didn't know whether to laugh or be angry. 'But you should have told me; I might have changed my mind...'

'No, no. You married me, not my family. You'll like them. We don't see much of each other but we like each other.'

'This is a ridiculous conversation,' said Eulalia severely.

He tucked her hand under his arm. 'Yes, isn't it? Let us go home for tea and then I must do some work, much though I regret that. You can make a list of your shopping while I'm doing that and I'll tell you where the best shops are.'

They had tea in the drawing room by the fire—English tea and crumpets.

'Can you get crumpets here?' asked Eulalia, licking a buttery finger.

'There is a shop which sells them, I believe. We don't, as a nation, have afternoon tea, only if we go to a café or tea room.'

'Am I going to find life very different here?'

He thought for a moment. 'No, I think not. You will soon have friends, and there are any number of English living here. I shall take you to the hospital and introduce you to my colleagues there and their wives will invite you for coffee.'

'Oh—but not before I've got some new clothes...'

'No, no. In any case I shall be away for a couple of days next week; I have to go to

Rome.'

'Rome? To operate?'

'To examine students. Ko will take care of you.'

He had sounded casual and for some reason she felt hurt. Surely she could have gone with him or he could have refused to go?

An unreasonable wish, she realised.

He went away to his study presently and she found pencil and paper and made a list of the clothes she might need. The list got longer and longer and finally she became impatient with it and threw it on the table by her chair. What was the use of making a list if she had no idea of how much money she could spend?

She curled up in her chair and went to sleep. It had been an active day and, besides that, her thoughts were in a muddle.

When she awoke Aderik was sitting on a nearby chair with Humbert pressed close to him, reading the list.

He glanced at her and finished his reading. 'You will need more than two evening frocks and a good handful of what my sisters call little dresses. There will be coffee mornings and tea parties. You'll need a raincoat and hat—there's a Burberry shop.'

He took out his pen and added to the list. 'If you'd rather not go alone Ko will go with you, show you where the best shops are and wait while you shop.'

'The best man,' said Eulalia. 'You said he had a wife—Daisy...'

'They had a son two weeks ago. When I get back from Rome we'll go and visit them. I dare say she will go shopping with you if you would like that.'

'If she could spare the time, I would.'

'We will have a day out tomorrow, but will you come to church with me after breakfast?'

'Yes, of course I will. Is it that little church we pass on the way here?'

'Yes; there is service at nine o'clock. I think you may find it not so very different from your own church.'

Eulalia, standing beside him in the ancient, austere little church, reflected that he was quite right. Of course she couldn't understand a word but somehow that didn't matter. And afterwards the *dominee* and several people gathered round to meet her, making her feel instantly at home. That Aderik was well liked and respected among the congregation was obvious, and it struck her anew how little she knew about him.

They went back home for coffee and then, with Humbert on the back seat, set off on their tour.

Mr van der Leurs, a man of many parts,

had planned the day carefully. He took the road to Apeldoorn and then by side roads to Zwolle and then north for another twenty miles to Blokzijl, a very small town surrounding a harbour on the inland lakes of the region. It was hardly a tourist centre but the restaurant by the lock was famous for its food. He parked the car and as Eulalia got out she exclaimed, 'Oh, how Dutch! Look at the ducks and that little bridge over the lock.'

She beamed up at him. 'This is really Holland, isn't it?'

'Yes. In the summer there are yachts going to and fro and it can be crowded. Would you like to have lunch here?'

'Oh, yes, please...'

They had a table in a window overlooking the lock in a room half full of people, and Eulalia, with one eye on the scene outside, discovered that she was hungry and ate prawns, grilled sole and Charlotte Russe with a splendid appetite, listening to Aderik's gentle flow of conversation, feeling quietly happy.

They didn't hurry over their meal but presently they drove on, still going north in the direction of Leeuwarden, driving around the lakes and then to Sneek and Bolsward before bypassing Leeuwarden and crossing over to North Holland on the other side of the Ijsselmeer. The dyke road was almost empty of traffic, just over eighteen miles of it, and Mr van der Leurs put his well-shod foot down. Eulalia barely had time to get her bearings before they were on land again, and making for Alkmaar.

They stopped for tea then but they didn't linger over it. 'I'm going to take the coast road as far as Zandvoort. If it's not too dark we'll take a look at the sea.'

The road was a short distance from the sea but very soon he turned off to Egmond aan Zee, a small seaside town, very quiet now that it was winter. He parked the car and together they went down to the beach. It was dusk now, with a grey sky and a rough sea. Eulalia could see the sands stretching away north and south into the distance. 'You could walk for miles,' she said, then added, 'I like it; it's lonely...'

'Now it is. In the summer the beach is packed.'

He took her arm. 'Come, it will be dark very soon. We'll be home in half an hour.'

It was quite dark by the time they got home, to sit by the fire and then eat their supper while Aderik patiently answered her questions about everything she had seen during the day.

It was lovely, she reflected, sitting there in the beautiful drawing room with Aderik in his chair and Humbert sprawled between them. Despite the grandeur of the room, she felt as though she belonged. She was sleepy too and presently he said, 'Go to bed, my dear; we've had quite a long day.'

'When do you have to go tomorrow?'

'I must leave the house by half past seven.'

'May I come and have breakfast with you? You won't mind if I'm in my dressing gown?'

'That would be delightful. Shall I tell Mekke to call you at seven o'clock?'

'Yes, please, and thank you for a lovely day.' They went to the door together. 'I feel as though I've been here for years and years.' She gave a little laugh, 'That's silly, isn't it? We've only been married a couple of days.'

He smiled and kissed her cheek. 'Sleep well.'

The house was quiet when she went down in the morning but there were lights on in the dining room and a shaded lamp in the hall. She slid into her chair opposite Aderik, wished him 'Good morning' and told him not to get up. She was wearing the same worthy dressing gown, he saw at once, and her hair was hanging down her back and she was flushed with sleep and very beautiful. He hoped it wouldn't be too long before she fell in love with him...

She asked about his trip and he answered her briefly, promising to phone her that evening. When he got up to go his goodbye was cheerful and brief; nothing of his longing to stay with her showed in his face, which was very calm. She had been happy with him during their two days together: he had seen that in her expressive face—now she would be alone and have time to think about them and realise how happy they had been—and miss him.

It was a gamble, and Mr van der Leurs wasn't a gambling man. But he had faith in his own judgement and a great deal of patience.

He said, 'Ko will take care of you,' and kissed her swiftly, leaving her standing in the hall feeling quite lost.

But not for long. When she came down presently, dressed and ready for the day ahead, Ko was waiting for her. He handed her an envelope and went away to fetch some coffee and she sat down and opened it. There was a great deal of money inside. There was a note too from Aderik. 'Buy as much as you want; if you need more money, ask Ko who will know where to get it.'

She began counting the notes. It seemed like a fortune; she would have to make another list and plan what she could buy. Whatever she did buy would have to be of the best quality. Her coat was of the finest cashmere and she guessed expensive, but Aderik hadn't quibbled over its price. Whatever she bought must match it. She stowed the money away carefully and, seen on her way by a fatherly Ko, left the house.

Years of penny-pinching had taught her to be a careful shopper and that stood her in good stead now, as she stifled an impulse to enter the first elegant boutique she saw and buy everything which might take her fancy. Instead she sought out some of the bigger stores, inspecting their windows, and presently chose one bearing a resemblance to one of the fashion houses in London and went inside.

She had made a wise choice; the underwear department had everything a well-dressed girl would want. She choked over the prices but even though Aderik was never likely to see her purchases she would feel right. And there was no reason why he shouldn't see a dressing gown—she bought a pink quilted silk garment almost too charming to keep hidden in the bedroom and added it to the pile of silk and lace.

When she had paid for them and asked for them to be delivered to the house, there was still a great deal of money left...

Aderik had told her to buy a Burberry. She found the shop, bought it and added a matching rain hat, paid for those too and arranged to have them delivered. With the bit firmly between her teeth, she went in search of the boutique where Aderik had bought her coat.

The saleslady recognised her at once. She was alone? she enquired of Eulalia. 'Perhaps mevrouw is looking for something special to wear of an evening, ready for the festive season?'

'Well, yes, but first I'd like to see some dresses for the day. Thin wool or jersey?'

'I have just the thing.' The saleslady raised her voice and said something unintelligible to a young girl hovering at the back of the boutique, who sped away and returned presently with several dresses.

'A perfect size twelve,' said the saleslady in her more or less fluent English, 'and a figure to make other women envious, *mevrouw*. Try this jersey dress, such a good colour—we call it mahogany— very simple in cut but elegant enough to wear later in the day.'

An hour later, Eulalia left the boutique, considerably lighter in purse but possessed of a jersey dress, a cashmere twin set, a tweed suit, its skirt short enough to show off her shapely legs, a dark red velvet dress which she was advised could be worn on any occasion after six o'clock, and a pleated skirt, all of which would be delivered to the house. She had tried on several evening gowns too, uncertain which to buy. It was the saleslady who suggested that perhaps she might like to return when it was convenient and bring her husband with her.

Eulalia had agreed although she doubted if he would have the time or the inclination to go with her, but at least she could describe them to him and he could advise her.

She went home for her lunch then; tomorrow was another day and she needed to sit down quietly and check her list and count her money. But first of all after lunch she would put on her coat again and go with Ko and Humbert to Vondel Park and walk there for an hour while Humbert nosed around happily.

There weren't many people about when they got there for it was cold and the day was closing in but she enjoyed it; Ko had ready answers to all her questions, giving gentle advice, telling her a little about the household's routine.

'And Katje hopes that you will come to the kitchen when you wish; she is anxious that you should know everything. You have only to say when you wish it.'

'I'd like that very much, Ko. When is the best time? I mean, Katje has her work to do.'

'That is thoughtful of you, *mevrouw*. Perhaps in the afternoon after lunch?'

'Tomorrow? You will be there, Ko, to translate…?'

'Naturally, *mevrouw*. Now it is time for us to return.'

The parcels and boxes had been delivered while they had been in the park; Eulalia had her tea by the fire and then went upstairs and unpacked everything and put them in drawers and cupboards. She would go to bed early, she decided, and try on everything then.

It was as she was sitting in the drawing room with Humbert pressed up against her that she began to feel lonely. The excitement of shopping had kept her

thoughts busy all day but now she wished that Aderik was there. Even if he was working in his study, just to know that he was at home would be nice. They really got on very well, she reflected. Of course they had to get to know each other, and since it seemed that he was away from home a good deal that may take some time. In the meantime she must learn her way around and be the kind of wife he wished for. He would be home again tomorrow—late in the evening, he had said, but she would wait up for him as any good wife would.

He phoned later that evening and she gave a sigh of relief at the sound of his voice.

'You have had a happy day?' he wanted to know.

She told him briefly. It would have been nice to have described her shopping to him in some detail but after a day's work he might not appreciate that. 'I've had a lovely day and Ko took me and Humbert to Vondel Park this afternoon. Have you been busy?'

'Yes. I shall have to stay another day, I'm afraid. I'll ring you tomorrow and let you know at what time I'll be home.'

She tried to keep the disappointment out of her voice. She said, 'Take care, won't you?'

'Yes, and you too. *Tot ziens*.'

It was raining the next morning but that

couldn't dampen Eulalia's determination to do some more shopping. In the Burberry and the little hat she went in search of boots and shoes. She had seen what she wanted on the previous day in a shop in the Kalverstraat—boots, soft leather with a sensible heel, and plain court shoes, black, and, since she could afford it, brown as well. She would need more than these but the boots were expensive and she needed gloves...

Her purchases made, she went into a café and ordered coffee and then walked home, getting lost on the way. Not that she minded; she was bound to miss her way until she had lived in Amsterdam for some time. She had a tongue in her head and everyone seemed to speak English...

After lunch she went to the kitchen and sat down at the big scrubbed table with Ko and Katje. It was a room after her own heart, with a flagstone floor, old-fashioned wooden armchairs on either side of the Aga and a great wooden dresser with shelves loaded with china. There were cupboards too and Katje showed her the pantry, the boot room and the laundry and a narrow staircase behind a door in the wall.

It was a delightful room, and she sat there feeling very much at home, realising that it was her home now.

The afternoon passed quickly, looking into cupboards with Katje, going round the house once more, examining piles of linen stacked in vast cupboards, being shown where the keys of the house were kept, the wine cellar, the little room where Ko kept the silver locked up.

She had her tea presently, had a long telephone talk with Tom and Pam and then had her dinner. Aderik had said that he would phone and she went back to the drawing room to wait for his call. When he did ring it was almost eleven o'clock and he had little to say, only that he would be home in the late afternoon.

Eulalia put the phone down feeling let down and then she told herself that she was being a fool. Aderik had probably had a hard day; the last thing he wanted to do was to listen to her chatter. And he was coming home tomorrow.

Just before she slept she decided to wear the jersey dress. 'It will really be very nice to see him again,' she muttered sleepily. 'I hope he feels the same about me.'

She woke in the night with the terrible thought that he might not like having her for his wife after all but in the sane light of morning she had forgotten it.

Continues on page 58

ACROSS

1. 1966 film adaptation of Joy Adamson book (4,4)
6. 1967 Rex Harrison part (2,8)
13. Spacious
14. Motor oil
15. Animal control group (Abbr.)
16. Oft filmed Dicken's tale (5,12)
18. Fib
19. Camille actress Talmadge
21. Surrey town
23. Manipulate
25. Young female horse
27. Used for making meringues (3,6)
29. Disinfest
30. Fund
31. Nightmare, for one

32. Sharp
33. Vipers
35. Moral principle
38. Sinews
39. Comic Costello
40. 1946 Cary Grant espionage flick
42. Broadcast medium
43. Newt
44. Play
46. Artist's tool
47. Propose
49. 1987 Nicholson fantasy, with The (7,2,8)
54. Tough fabric
55. Mulling over
56. Heartbeat
57. Oft filmed Blackmore novel (5,5)
58. 1983 Streep film

DOWN

2. Colourless gas
3. Negative response
4. Loosen up
5. Crests or ensigns
6. Float
7. Fatigued, to the hilt (4-5)
8. Game of chance
9. 1983 MacLaine, Nicholson flick (5,2,10)
10. Coat feature
11. 1944 film of Pearl Buck tale (6,4)
12. Oft-filmed Bronte novel (4,4)
17. 1941 Vivien Leigh, Laurence Olivier romancer (4,8,5)
20. Returned to a former state

21. Consume
22. Red Planet
24. Presents
26. Formal daytime meals
28. Title
32. Discernment
34. Before beam or light
36. 1969 Burt Lancaster WWII flick (6,4)
37. Pound
38. 1990 Cher comedy
39. Grab hold of (5,4)
41. Assam
45. Social functions
48. Smooth-skinned tropical fruit
50. Recorded
51. Soft leather
52. Spiritual being
53. Eskimo hut
56. Church bench

SU DOKU

To solve a **Su Doku** puzzle fill in all the squares in the grid so that each row, column and each of the 3x3 'inner squares' contains the numbers 1 to 9.

6	1	4		2	5		9	
	5			9	6	4		
	9	3		4	8	6		
9	3	6	4	8	1		7	
	4		6	3	2	8	1	9
1	8	2	9	5	7	3	4	6
	6		8		4			
4	2		5		9			
	7		2		3			4

ARROW WORD

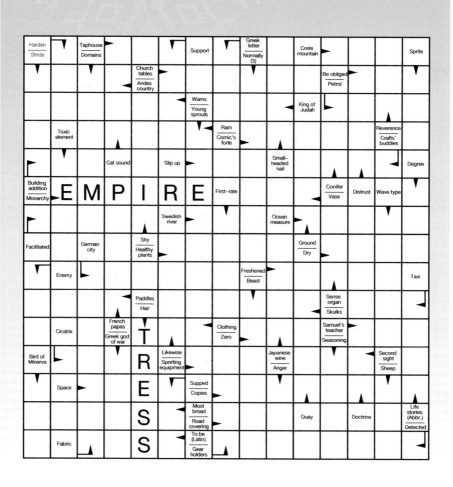

The ARROW WORD puzzle grid contains the following clue cells and answers:

Harden / Stride	▼	Taphouse / Domains			▼	Support	▼	Greek letter / Normally (3)		Crete mountain	▶				Sprite
▼		▼	Church tables / Andes country	▶					▼		Be obliged / Petrol	▶			▼
	Toxic element				Warns / Young sprouts		Ram / Comic's forte	▶		King of Judah	▶			Reverence / Crafts' buddies	
▶	▼		Cat sound		Slip up	▶	▼		Small-headed nail		▲		▲		Degree
Building addition / Monarchy	▶ E	M	P	I	R	E	First-rate	▼			Conifer / Vase	Distrust	Wave type	▼	
▶		▲	Swedish river	▶					Ocean measure		▶		▼		
Facilitated		German city	Shy / Healthy plants	▶						Ground / Dry	▶				
▼	Enemy	▶					Freshened / Beast	▶			▲			Taxi	
		▲	Paddles / Hair				▼		Sense organ / Skulks	◀				◀	
	Cicatrix	French papas / Greek god of war	T		Clothing / Zero	▶	▲		Samuel's teacher / Seasoning	▶				
Bird of Minerva	▶	▼	R	Likewise / Sporting equipment			Japanese wine / Anger		▼		◀	Second sight / Sheep		
▼	Space	▶	E	▼	Supped / Copies	▶			▼		▲		▲	
			S	Most broad / Road covering				Quay		Doctrine		Life stories (Abbr.) / Detected	
	Fabric	▲	S	To be (Latin) / Gear holders	◀							◀	

Solutions on page 174

IT WAS wet and cold and very windy in the morning. Eulalia was glad that she had done all the shopping she had planned to do and needed little persuasion from Ko to stay indoors. She peered out at the dismal weather and hoped that Aderik would have a good journey home. It was a pity that he hadn't told her if he was likely to arrive earlier. She got into the jersey dress, did her face with extra care and arranged her hair just so before going to the library to wander round its shelves with Humbert for company. She drank her coffee, going every now and then to look out of the window to see if the Bentley was outside.

There was still no sign of it as she ate her lunch and since sitting around waiting was pointless she set off to explore the house again. This time she went to the very top floor and discovered the attics—two rooms under the gabled roof with tiny windows back and front. They were filled with tables and chairs, old pictures, boxes of china and glass and long-forgotten children's toys. There were great leather trunks too; she hauled on their lids and discovered dresses of a bygone age carefully wrapped in tissue paper.

Someone had left a pinny hanging on a door and she put it on for the rooms were dusty and sat down on one of the trunks to examine a large box filled with toys, while Humbert, bored, went to sleep on a pile of rugs.

Mr van der Leurs, coming silently into his house, got no further than the hall before Ko came to meet him, took his coat and his overnight case and offered him coffee or a meal. He wanted neither but took his briefcase to his study and asked, '*Mevrouw* is home? It seems very quiet...'

'She was in the library but I believe she went upstairs.' He added, 'Humbert was with her – devoted he is, already.'

Mr van der Leurs went up the staircase; for such a big man he was light on his feet and quiet. He paused on the landing for his ear had caught a faint sound from somewhere above him.

He went on up to the next floor and then opened the small door in a wall which led to the narrow stairs to the attics. It was cold up there, for which reason Eulalia had closed the door at the top of the stairs, and as he opened it Humbert hurled himself at him. Mr van der Leurs stood for a moment, the great dog in his arms, staring over his head at Eulalia, as she got to her feet, hampered by the armful of dolls she was holding. She put them down carefully, beaming at him.

'Aderik, you're home...' She took off the

pinny. 'I meant to be sitting in the drawing room looking welcoming, only you didn't come so I came up here to pass the time and now I'm a bit dusty.'

Words which brought a gleam to his eye but all he said was, 'How very nice you look; is that a new dress?' He crossed the room and kissed her, a friendly kiss conveying nothing of his feelings. 'How delightful it is to be home again.'

'It's almost tea time but would you like a meal? Did you have a good flight and was the visit to Rome successful?'

'Shall we have tea round the fire and I'll tell you about my trip?'

'Oh, please. I'll just put these dolls back...'

They went back down to the drawing room with Humbert at their heels and found Ko arranging the tea tray before the fire. Since Katje had a poor opinion of the meals Mr van der Leurs was offered when he was away from home, there was a splendid selection of tiny sandwiches, hot crumpets in their lidded dish, currant bread and butter and a Madeira cake—Katje considered that she made the finest Madeira cake in Amsterdam.

Over tea and for an hour or more after, he told her where he had been and why, what he had done and where he had stayed. Listening to his quiet voice gave her the pleasant feeling that they had been married for years, completely at ease with each other and like any other married couple.

'I don't need to go to hospital today,' said Aderik. 'Would you like to meet Daisy? Jules will probably be at home too.'

'Yes, please. Jules looked very nice and I'd like to meet Daisy.'

The der Huizmas lived less than ten minutes' walk away and it was bright and cold. Walking through narrow streets, crossing canals by narrow bridges with Humbert walking sedately beside them, Eulalia asked, 'They don't mind Humbert coming too?'

'No, they have a dog—Bouncer; he and Humbert are the greatest of friends.'

As they mounted the steps to the front door Eulalia saw that the house was very similar to Aderik's but she had no time to look around before the door was opened.

'Joop,' Mr van der Leurs greeted the severe-looking man, who stood aside so that they might enter. 'We're expected? Eulalia, this is Joop who runs the house with Jette, his wife.'

'My wife, Joop.'

Eulalia offered a hand and watched the severe elderly face break into a smile before he led the way across the hall to a door which was flung open before they reached it.

The girl who came to meet them was small, with no pretensions to good looks, but her smile was lovely.

Aderik gave her a hug and kissed her soundly. 'Daisy, I've brought Eulalia as I promised.' He turned to greet Jules who had followed his wife.

Daisy took Eulalia's hand. 'You're as beautiful as Aderik said you were. I do hope we shall be friends...'

'I'm sure we shall.' Eulalia was kissed in her turn by Jules who took her coat and hat and urged her into the drawing room. All this while Humbert had been sitting, quivering with impatience, and once in the room he went to greet the rather odd-looking dog who came trotting to meet him. 'Bouncer,' explained Daisy.

Jules added, 'A dog of many ancestors but devoted to all of us as well as Humbert. Come and sit by the fire and tell us what you have been doing since you arrived.'

They talked over their coffee and biscuits and then the two men went to Jules's study and the dogs with them.

'So now shall we go and see Julius? He's three weeks old today. He'll be asleep because I've just fed him. Jules's sister's nanny came to help me for a while but I want to look after him myself—and Jules is marvellous with him.'

She led the way upstairs into a large airy room. There was an elderly woman sitting in a chair knitting who smiled and nodded at them as they went in to bend over the cot.

Julius was sleeping, a miniature of his

father, and Daisy said, 'Isn't he gorgeous? We had to call him Julius after Jules's father but it's a nice name, don't you think?'

'Just right for him; he's a lovely boy. You must be so proud of him.'

Eulalia looked at the sleeping baby, thinking she would like one just like him...

Perhaps in a while Aderik would become fond of her—she knew he liked her otherwise he wouldn't have married her, but he treated her as a dear friend and that wasn't the same. He hadn't mentioned love—it was she who had done that and his answer had been almost casual.

Later, on their way back to the house, Eulalia said, 'They're happy, aren't they? Jules and Daisy—how did they meet?'

'Daisy came to Amsterdam to see about some antiques and fell into a canal, and Jules fished her out—they had met in England at her father's antiques shop but I imagine her ducking started the romance.'

'He must love her very dearly—I mean, I don't suppose Daisy looked too glamorous...'

He said evenly, 'I don't imagine that glamour has much to do with falling in love.'

'Well, no, but I should think it might help...'

Next morning they had breakfast together and he left the house directly they had finished, saying he wasn't sure when he would be home. She decided she would go to the shops and get something to do— knitting or tapestry work. Until she knew some people time would hang heavily on her hands. Of course when Aderik had the time he would introduce her to his family and friends...

A question which was partly settled when he got home that evening.

'It will be the feast of St Nikolaas in a day or two,' he told her. 'You will have seen the shops... St Nikolaas comes to the hospital and perhaps you would like to come and see him? It would be a good opportunity for you to meet some of my colleagues there with their wives and children. It's something of an occasion, especially for the children.'

'I'd like that. What time does he come?'

'Eleven o'clock. I'll come and fetch you about half past ten.' He smiled at her. 'I think you'll enjoy it. The day after tomorrow.'

She saw him only briefly the next day for he left the house directly after breakfast. It was evening before he came home and then after dinner he went to his study. When, feeling peevish, she went to wish him goodnight he made no effort to keep her talking.

At breakfast he reminded her to be ready when he came for her.

'You are sure you want me to come?'

She sounded tart and he looked up from the letter he was reading to stare at her.

'Quite sure,' he told her mildly. 'Everyone's looking forward to meeting you.'

Which she decided wasn't a very satisfactory answer.

But she took care to be ready for him and she had taken great pains with her appearance—the new coat, one of the new dresses, the little hat just so on her dark hair, good shoes and handbag. She hoped that she looked exactly as the wife of a respected member of the medical profession should look.

It seemed that she did for when Aderik came into the house he gave her a long, deliberate look and said quietly, 'I'm proud of my wife, Lally.'

She said breathlessly, 'Oh, are you really, Aderik? What a nice thing to say. I'm feeling a bit nervous.'

'No need.' He spoke casually, popped her into the car and drove to the hospital.

Its forecourt was filled with people, mostly children. He parked in the area reserved for the senior consultants and took her into the vast foyer through a side door. There was a crowd round the entrance but there were small groups of people standing and chatting at the back. Eulalia reminded herself that she was no longer the canteen lady and took comfort from Aderik's hand under her elbow and found herself shaking hands with the hospital director and his wife and then a seemingly endless succession of smiling faces and firm handshakes. And Daisy was there with Jules.

'Hello, you do look nice. What did you think of the director and his wife?'

'Friendly; he looks awfully nice and kind and so does his wife.'

'They are. You do know that she is English?' And at Eulalia's surprised look Daisy added, 'Husbands do forget things, don't they? She came over here to nurse, oh, years ago, and they got married and they're devoted to each other. They've got four children, three boys and a girl. Her name's Christina. She's forty-five. She gives lovely dinner parties and we all like her very much.'

She beamed at Eulalia. 'You will be very happy here and Aderik is a dear. We're all so glad that he's found you. You will get asked out a lot, you know.'

The men had joined them and everyone was moving forward to get a good view. St Nikolaas was approaching; they could hear the children shouting and clapping and a moment later Eulalia saw him seated on his white horse, in his bishop's robes, riding into the forecourt with his attendant, Zwarte Piet, running beside him, the sack into which he would put all the naughty children over his shoulder.

The noise was terrific as he got off his

horse and stood in the forecourt, an impressive figure who presently addressed his audience in a long speech. Eulalia didn't understand a word but she found it fascinating and when he had finished clapped and cheered as loudly as anyone there.

St Nikolaas came into the foyer then, making his stately way towards the children's wards. He paused to speak to the director, nodded graciously to everyone as he passed and disappeared into one of the lifts with the director and his wife.

Aderik took her arm. 'He will be about half an hour and then he comes back to the courtyard and throws sweets to the children there. We're going to have lunch now—another opportunity for you to get to know everyone.'

He glanced down at her happy face. 'Enjoying it?'

'Oh, yes. Does he go anywhere else?'

'The other hospitals in Amsterdam. Of course there is a St Nikolaas in every town and village. It's a great occasion for the children for he leaves presents for them by the fireplace in their homes and if a grown-up finds a gift by his plate he mustn't ask who it is from but thank St Nikolaas for it. Now if you're ready we'll go and have lunch.'

A buffet had been set up in the consultants' room, a vast apartment furnished solidly with a great deal of brown leather and dark wood. Chairs and tables had been set up and everybody fetched their food and found places to sit with friends.

Mr van der Leurs piled a plate of food for Eulalia, settled her at a table with Daisy, the casualty officer's wife and two younger doctors, promised to be back shortly and went away. The doctors were friendly, only too pleased to tell her about St Nikolaas and Zwarte Piet, and she began to enjoy herself.

Presently they were joined by an older man who introduced himself as Pieter Hirsoff, one of the anaesthetists. He was charming to Eulalia and she responded rather more warmly than she realised. It was pleasant to be chatted up... When he suggested that she might like to see one of the many museums in the city, she agreed readily. 'But not the Rijksmuseum,' she told him. 'Aderik has promised to take me there.'

'I know just the right one for you—a patrician house furnished just as it was when it was first built. It's on one of the *grachten*. Suppose I come for you tomorrow afternoon? I'm sure you will enjoy it.'

He excused himself then and Eulalia joined in the general talk, wondering where Aderik had got to.

He came presently with Jules. They had been up to their wards, they explained, and St Nikolaas was about to leave.

'I'll drive you home,' he told Eulalia, 'but I must come back here for a while.'

Daisy said quickly, 'Come back with us, Eulalia, and have tea. Jules has to come back here and I'd love a gossip. Aderik can fetch you when he's finished here.'

So Eulalia went back to the der Huizmas' and had tea with Daisy and talked about the morning's events. Baby Julius was brought down to be fed and then lay placidly sleeping on Eulalia's lap while they discussed Christmas.

'We go to Jules's family home and so do the rest of his family. It's great fun. I dare say you'll go to Aderik's family. You haven't met them yet?'

'No. There wasn't much time to arrange anything before we married and Aderik doesn't have much free time.'

> **CHRISTMAS TIP**
> Don't throw away tree decorations that are missing hooks or caps – if they are arranged in a glass bowl they look stunning as the centrepiece of a table.

'Oh, well,' said Daisy comfortably. 'You'll see them all at Christmas. Now you've met everyone at the hospital you'll make lots of friends, but I hope we'll be friends, real friends, you and me.'

It was later that evening as Eulalia and Aderik sat together after dinner that she told him she was going to spend the afternoon with Dr Hirsoff.

Mr van der Leurs had been reading his paper, but now he put it down.

'Which museum are you going to?' He sounded only mildly interested, and when she told him he said, 'Ah, yes, an interesting place. You liked him?'

'Yes. He's very amusing and easy to talk to.' She looked up sharply. 'You don't like him?'

'My dear girl, what has that to do with it? You are free to choose your friends and I would never stand in your way. We are both, I trust, sensible people, tolerant of each other's tastes and wishes. I hope you will have a very pleasant afternoon.'

He turned a page and returned to his reading, leaving her seething although she had no idea why she was put out. She knew that their marriage wasn't quite like the normal matrimonial state but surely he should show some interest, concern even, in the friends she made.

Pieter Hirsoff came for her after lunch and, since Aderik had phoned to say that he wouldn't be home until the evening and she had spent the morning painstakingly discussing household matters with Katje and Ko, Eulalia was quite ready to enjoy his company. And he was good company, guiding her expertly through the museum and then suggesting that they might have a cup of tea before he drove her home. He took her to a large hotel on the Leidseplein and ordered tea and cakes, and it wasn't until she told him that she would like to go home that he put a hand over hers on the table and smiled across it at her.

'Eulalia, we must meet again. This afternoon has been delightful. We are two lonely people, are we not? My wife doesn't care to live in Amsterdam and Aderik is so engrossed in his work, I doubt if he is home as often as he might be.'

She was too surprised to speak for a moment. She might be twenty-seven years old but there hadn't been much chance to gain worldly experience behind the canteen counter... She quelled a desire to lean over and box his ears; that would never do! He was a colleague of Aderik's. She said in a matter-of-fact voice, 'I'm sorry you're lonely, but I'm not; I'm very happy. Aderik is a marvellous husband and I love living here. I know I shall make lots of friends—his friends too—and I'm sure you'll be one of them. It was kind of you to take me out and I've enjoyed it but now I really must go home.'

'I hope Aderik knows what a treasure he's married.' They were walking to the car. 'I'm a persistent man, Eulalia.'

In the car she said, 'You're being silly now. Aderik and I have only been married for little more than a week; can you not understand that life for us is perfect?'

Which wasn't quite true but surely she would be forgiven for the lie so that she could convince the man? She had thought she liked him, but now she wasn't so sure...

Mr van der Leurs didn't get home until almost dinner time. He came into the drawing room with Humbert, who had gone into the hall to meet him, and bade Eulalia a cheerful hello.

'Did you enjoy your afternoon with Hirsoff?' he wanted to know.

'Since you ask,' said Eulalia tartly, 'I didn't.'

He handed her a drink and asked, still cheerfully, 'Oh? Why not?'

'He got a bit, well, a bit intense...'

'What did you expect? You're a beautiful young woman. It's only logical that he would chat you up.'

She tossed off her sherry. 'What a simply beastly thing to say. And if you knew that he was that kind of a man, why didn't you tell me not to go out with him?'

He had picked up the first of his letters and slit the envelope carefully before he answered.

'When we married—before we married—I told you that you might have all the time you needed to get to know me and settle into your new life. I hope by now that you know that I meant what I said. The fact that we are married and like each other enough to live together doesn't mean that I have any right to dictate to you.'

'You mean that you would never

interfere in anything I might want to do or with the friends that I might make?'

'That is what I mean.'

'You don't mind?' she began angrily, and was interrupted by Ko telling them that dinner was served.

After that there was no chance to go on talking about it. Mr van der Leurs, keeping his thoughts to himself, rambled on about this and that, making it impossible for Eulalia to argue with him. After dinner he told her that he had some phone calls to make and it was an hour or more before he came back to sit by the fire with Humbert at his feet.

Eulalia sat with her newly bought tapestry frame before her, stabbing the needle in and out of the canvas, regardless of the havoc she was making. They were quarrelling, she reflected, or rather she was trying to quarrel; Aderik was being most annoyingly placid. She wondered what she would have to do to ruffle that smooth manner. She couldn't think of anything at the moment so she bade him a chilly goodnight and went to bed, her dignified exit rather spoilt by the kiss he dropped on her cheek as he opened the door for her.

She took a long time to go to sleep. She would have liked someone to confide in but the only person who would have done

nicely was Aderik and he, she had to admit, seemed placidly indifferent, rather like an elder brother who didn't want to be bothered but was tolerant of her.

And how absurd, she reflected, half asleep by now, discussing her doubts and worries with the very person who was causing them.

An opinion that was strengthened at breakfast the next morning; Aderik was his usual amiable self but quite clearly he had neither the time nor the inclination to enter into a serious discussion.

He handed her an envelope addressed to them both. 'An invitation to the Christmas ball in a week's time. The invitation was delayed until we returned here but it was taken for granted that we would accept. Send a note to Christina ter Brandt, will you? It's a grand affair...'

'I haven't a dress...'

'Then we will go and buy one. Tomorrow directly after lunch.'

He was looking through his post. 'There are several invitations to dine and here's a letter for you inviting you to have coffee with Christina...'

He added warmly, 'You'll like her: everyone does.' He got up. 'I must go—I've a full day ahead of me so don't expect me until this evening. Why not do some Christmas shopping? Perhaps you can think of something to give Katje—and Mekke is getting engaged. I'll see to Ko.'

'And your family?'

'I'll take a morning off and we'll go shopping together.'

He kissed her cheek swiftly as he went.

Leaving her with a great deal to think about. His family would come to stay at Christmas, he had told her that, but somehow she hadn't thought any more about it. Now Christmas was less than three weeks away; there would be presents to buy and Katje to consult about meals and rooms. She choked back indignation; he had told her so little...

She sought out Ko. 'Christmas,' she said urgently. 'People will be coming to visit. How long do they stay, Ko? And do we have a tree and holly and give presents?'

He assured her that they did. Christmas, he told her in his careful English, had at one time been a rather solemn occasion, more a church festival, while St Nikolaas had been a more important feast. But Holland had adopted many English customs so that there would be turkey and Christmas pudding, a Christmas tree and decorations and the giving of presents.

'You will wish to consult with Katje, *mevrouw*, and decide on menus and beds for the guests. It will be a relief for *mijnheer* that he has you here to oversee the preparations.'

That evening after dinner, sitting comfortably together, it seemed a good time to her to broach the subject of Christmas.

'There is a great deal I need to know,' she began firmly, 'and I would like you to tell me.'

Mr van der Leurs put down his newspapers, the very picture of an attentive husband. 'Such as?'

'Well, your family. How many are coming to stay and for how long?' A sudden surge of indignation made her voice shrill. 'I know nothing about them.' She added pettishly, 'Probably they won't like me.'

Mr van der Leurs, at his most reasonable, observed, 'How can you say that when you haven't met them?' He saw that she was put out and added in a quite different voice, 'My mother is the kind of mother one hugs and kisses and who offers a cosy shoulder if one wants comforting. My sisters are younger than I am; Marijka is twenty-eight, married and has two children—boys. Lucia is thirty, married, also, with two girls and a boy. Paul is the youngest, twenty-three, in his last year at Leiden. He falls in and out of love so often I've given up trying to remember their names.'

He smiled then. 'Contrary to your expectations, they will like you and you will like them. They will come on Christmas Eve and Katje will be able to advise you as to where they will sleep and so on. I'll get a free morning and we'll go shopping together for presents. I believe that you will find it a Christmas very much like the celebrations in England.'

She had the lowering feeling that she had been making a fuss about nothing but there was still something. 'I have to buy a dress for the ball...'

'Tomorrow afternoon,' he reminded her placidly.

Not a very satisfactory conversation, she reflected; somehow she still felt that she had been making a fuss about nothing.

She went round the house in the morning with Katje, deciding which rooms should be made ready for their guests. There was time enough before Christmas but she wanted everything to be perfect...

Aderik was home punctually for lunch and while she went to put on her outdoor things he took Humbert for a brisk walk.

'And we'll walk too,' he told her. 'It's cold but dry and quicker than taking the car. Where do you want to go first?'

'The boutique where you bought my coat; there were some lovely dresses...'

She spent a blissful hour trying on one gown after another. It was hard to decide and she wanted to wear a dress which

Aderik would like. Finally she was left with a choice between a pearl-grey chiffon which fitted perfectly but was perhaps not quite grand enough, and a pale pink taffeta with a square neckline, tiny cap sleeves and a wide skirt. She tried them on again in turn and stood rather shyly while Aderik studied her.

'Have them both,' he decided.

While the saleswoman had gone to supervise their packing, Eulalia said in a whisper, 'But we're only going to one ball...'

'There will be others,' he said. He had got up from the elegant little chair and was wandering around, to stop by a stand upon which a russet velvet dress had been artfully thrown. 'Now, I like that. Will you try it on?'

The saleslady was already at his elbow. 'It is mevrouw's size and a perfect colour for her.'

So Eulalia was swept back behind the silk curtains and helped into the velvet dress and, studying her reflection in the long mirror, had to admit that she really looked rather nice in it...

'But when will I wear it?' she wanted to know as they gained the street once more.

'Christmas Day. Now come and help me choose something for my mother...'

Eulalia had coffee with Christina ter Brandt on the following morning. The ter Brandts lived in a large house in a tree-lined road on the outskirts of den Haag. Aderik had told her that when they were first married Duert ter Brandt had been director of the main hospital there but the last few years had seen him holding the same position in Amsterdam. It was more than half an hour's drive between the two cities but neither of them wished to leave their home in den Haag and Duert enjoyed driving.

Aderik had driven her there, going first to the hospital and coming back for her during the morning, and she had worried that he was wasting his time.

'Not when I'm with you, Lally,' he had told her quietly, 'but it might be a good idea if we were to look around for a car for you. Can you drive?'

'No. We never had a car.'

'Then you shall have lessons. I like to drive you myself but there may be occasions when that's not possible.'

He had stayed only a few minutes at the house and Christina had told him that she would be going into Amsterdam to have lunch with Duert and would see Eulalia safely home.

Eulalia enjoyed her morning; Christina was the kind of person one could confide in. Not that she did that but she was sure if she ever needed help or advice Christina would give it without fuss. And during the course of the morning she offered tidbits of information about the small everyday problems Eulalia had encountered.

'Of course Aderik will have told you a great deal but men do tend to overlook the small problems—tipping and tram fares and whether to wear a long or short dress; that kind of thing.'

Which reminded Eulalia to ask about the ball.

'Quite an event,' said Christina. 'Long dresses and any jewellery you can lay hands on...' She glanced quickly at Eulalia's hands, bare save for her wedding ring. 'It's all rather dignified and stately but great fun. You have met quite a few of the wives at the hospital? You'll meet a lot more but you'll only need to smile and murmur. You're rather a nine days' wonder, you know. Aderik's family are coming for Christmas? They always do; they're all delightful so don't worry about meeting them.'

> **DID YOU KNOW?**
> According to present-day astronomers the star of Bethlehem was not a star. They believe it was probably just a comet.

Christina poured more coffee. 'What do you think of the shops in Amsterdam?' she asked, and the conversation moved on.

She drove Eulalia back presently. 'I don't suppose Aderik will be back for lunch? It's been fun meeting you; you must come again and perhaps we can meet Daisy one morning here and have coffee?'

She drove away and Eulalia, warmed by her friendliness, had her lunch and then sat down to write Christmas cards and make a painstaking list of people for whom she would need to buy presents.

It seemed a good idea to go shopping the next day. Aderik would be away until mid-afternoon but if she had an early lunch she would have time to do at least some of her shopping—the children's presents, perhaps.

She went down to breakfast ready to tell him, to find that he had left the house in the early hours of the morning. An emergency, Ko told her, but he hoped to be home during the afternoon, probably around four o'clock.

So after lunch she set out with her list and a nicely filled purse. She felt at home in the city now although she was familiar only with the main streets. That morning, while she had been in the kitchen, she had told Katje that she was going shopping; it was surprising how well they understood each other as long as they kept their conversation to basics. Mekke had been there too, helping them out when they reached an impasse.

Her English was only a smattering but she was quick to understand and quick to learn.

When Eulalia had mentioned that she wanted to buy toys for the children she had told Eulalia where to go: a large store near the Central Station. *Mevrouw* must take a tram to the station and then walk; the shop was close by and she would find all the toys she could wish for there. She had even drawn a map to make finding it easy.

Eulalia clutched it as she walked to the Leidsestraat and got into a tram. It took her a few minutes to find the street Mekke had written down and when she reached the shop it was packed with people so that it took her longer than she expected to find just what she wanted.

The final purchases made, she glanced at her watch. Aderik would be home in a short while and she wanted to be there. She joined the surge of people leaving the store and started walking briskly, confident of her direction.

She had been walking for several minutes when it dawned on her that she was in a street she didn't know. Somehow she must have missed a turning. Not a serious matter, she told herself, and turned to walk back the way she had come. It was a narrow street and there were few people in it and no shops.

She stopped the first person coming towards her and asked the way; her Dutch was negligible but 'Central Station' and an arm waved enquiringly should be enough. It seemed that it wasn't; she tried two more people and was about to try again when the faint drizzle became a downpour. She was brushed aside; no one wanted to hang around answering questions in such weather...

There was no shelter and she could hardly knock on a door, while to try and find her way on her own was a waste of time... She wasn't the Colonel's granddaughter for nothing; she walked on until she saw a telephone box.

It took time to find the right coins and decipher the instructions, and, although there was no one about, the street outside, its lights almost obscured by the rain, looked menacing. She dialled and heard Aderik's voice.

'It's me. I'm lost and it's raining...'

He was reassuringly calm. 'Do you know the name of the street?'

'No, it's dark and—and empty.'

Mr van de Leurs, stifling a panic which astonished him, became all at once briskly reassuring.

'You're in a phone box? Tell me the number on the dial. Did you tell anyone where you were going?'

'Yes, Mekke. To a big toy shop near the station...' 'Stay where you are, Lally. I'll be with you very shortly.' 'I'm sorry to be a nuisance...' Her voice had a decided squeak. 'You've been very sensible, my dear; just stay where you are.'

Mr van der Leurs went into the hall and found Ko.

'Ask Mekke to come here, will you?'

When she came, he asked, 'Mekke, this shop you suggested *mevrouw* should visit—which street?' And when she told him he went on, 'And is there another entrance?'

'Yes, *mijnheer*, at the back of the shop.' She put her hand to her mouth. 'Mevrouw has lost herself?'

'Only temporarily. Do you know the street? Is there a phone box in it?'

'Yes. Turn left as you leave the shop.'

Mr van der Leurs nodded, whistled to Humbert and went out to his car. The streets were jammed with traffic but he knew a number of back ways...

He slid to a halt by the phone box and got out, opened its door and took Eulalia in his arms.

'My poor dear, you're wet and cold...'

'I was getting frightened too,' muttered Eulalia into his shoulder. 'I don't know why I got lost...'

'There was another entrance at the back of the shop—a natural mistake.'

He gathered up her parcels and shoved her gently into the car. 'Humbert's in the back.'

The car was warm and comfortable and Humbert pushed his woolly head against her shoulder. Eulalia supposed it was relief which made her want to cry. She sniffed away the tears and Aderik, without looking at her, said cheerfully, 'Dry clothes and tea and then you can show me what you have bought.'

PART FIVE

BACK at the house, Aderik pulled off her wet gloves, took off her coat and gave it to a hovering Ko and tossed her hat into a chair while Katje and Mekke, both talking at once, urged her to get into something warm.

'I'm only a bit wet,' protested Eulalia, and shivered.

'You appear half drowned. Go and get into something dry; your feet are sopping. And don't be long; I want my tea.'

So she went up to her room with an emotional Mekke in attendance, declaring in a mixture of English and Dutch that it was all her fault; she should never have told mevrouw to go to that shop. If mevrouw caught cold she would never forgive herself...

Ten minutes later Eulalia went back downstairs. Mekke had taken away her wet shoes and damp skirt and she had got into a jersey dress, brushed her hair and done her face, none the worse for her soaking. She had been frightened; she hoped that Aderik hadn't noticed that...

But of course he had.

He was standing with his back to the fire, his hands in his pockets and Humbert lolling beside him, while Ko arranged the tea things on a small round table between the two armchairs drawn up to the blaze.

Eulalia heaved a sigh of contentment; it was lovely to be home and she told him so. 'I'll be more careful next time,' she told him earnestly.

'It's easy to get lost,' he said easily, 'but you will soon find your way around. I must arrange for you to have lessons in Dutch so that you can ask the way. There are parts of Amsterdam where English might not be understood. I'm sorry that you got so wet...'

She had hoped that he might have said more than that; that it had been sensible of her to phone, a word of praise for her good sense and lack of panic, but he began a casual conversation about Christmas, dismissing the whole thing as trivial, reflected Eulalia pettishly.

Mr van der Leurs, watching her expressive face from under his eyelashes, thought his own thoughts and presently asked her if she would like to go shopping with him in the morning. 'I'm free until two o'clock; we might get the family presents bought. You found what you wanted for the children?'

'Yes. I hope they'll do; I mean, I haven't seen the children yet, have I? I don't know what they like.'

He didn't answer that but asked abruptly, 'Are you happy, Eulalia?'

She was too surprised to say anything for a moment. She put down the toasted teacake she was on the point of eating and licked a buttery finger. She said composedly, 'Yes, I am happy. Why do you ask, Aderik?'

'When I asked you to marry me I promised that you could have all the time you needed to get to know me and adjust to a new way of life. Ours was hardly a traditional marriage, was it? There should be time to reflect on the future together before becoming man and wife and I gave you no time for that. You may have regrets or doubts. And I think that you like me well enough to tell me if that is the case?'

She said thoughtfully, 'I don't think I ever had any doubts or regrets. Perhaps I should have thought about it more...but I feel at home here although it's much grander than I had expected. And I miss Grandfather...but we get on well together, don't we? And in a little while, as soon as I've learnt to speak Dutch and become the kind of wife you want...'

'You are the kind of wife I want, Lally. Stay just as you are. Learn to speak Dutch by all means, but don't change.'

He got up and pulled her gently to her feet. 'And now that you are quite certain that you are happy here with me I think that it is time we became engaged!'

He had put his arm around her shoulders and she stared up at him.

'Engaged? But we are married!'

'So now we will be engaged as well.'

He took a little box out of his pocket and opened it. There was a ring inside— diamonds in an old-fashioned gold setting. 'My grandmother's ring—I had it altered to fit your finger.'

He picked up her hand and slipped it above her wedding ring and, before she could speak, bent and kissed her. A gentle, slow kiss which left her with a surge of delight, so unexpected that she lost her breath.

'Oh,' said Eulalia, and kissed him back.

Mr van der Leurs' arms tightened around her for a moment, then he let her go. 'Sealed with a kiss,' he said lightly. 'Now tell me, have you any ideas about these presents?'

Eulalia sat down again, feeling vaguely disappointed, telling herself that she had no reason to be; hadn't Aderik just given her a most beautiful ring? And the kiss— she refused to think about that for the moment. It hadn't been like the other brief kisses he had given her—brief tokens of affection; it had left her feeling unsettled.

Mr van der Leurs, sitting in his chair, Humbert's great head resting on his knee, watched her face, and because he loved her so deeply he guessed her thoughts and was satisfied. A little more time and a lot more patience, he reflected.

They went shopping in the morning and Eulalia, at Aderik's quiet direction, bought silk scarves, exquisite handbags, gloves as

supple as velvet, earrings for his mother, thin gold bangles for his sisters, books for his brother, before having a cup of coffee while they decided what to get Katje, Ko and Mekke. Soft fleece-lined slippers for Ko, whose elderly feet would be glad of them at the end of the day, and silk-lined gloves for Katje. As for Mekke—a quilted dressing gown in one of the bright colours she loved...

They went home, well pleased with their purchases, and after an early lunch Aderik left for the hospital, leaving Eulalia sitting at the little writing desk in the small sitting room, carefully writing Christmas cards from the list he had given her. It was a long list, prudently updated from year to year so that all she had to do was copy names and addresses. Tomorrow, she decided, she would buy presents to send to England; the cards she had already sent. And she still had to find a present for Aderik.

The days passed surprisingly quickly, with last-minute presents to buy, Humbert to take for walks, and rather anxious preparations for the ball, now only a day or two away. And Aderik was seldom home before the early evening. So it was all the more delightful when she went down to breakfast on the morning before the day of the ball to be told that he was free until the afternoon and would she like to see more of Amsterdam?

'Not a museum; we'll save those for when we have hours of leisure. Suppose we just walk round some of the older streets? Most of them have little antique or book shops and the small houses are worth seeing.'

It was a day for walking: a cold blue sky, frost underfoot and the city bustling with preparations for Christmas. But the small streets to which Aderik led the way were quiet. The small gabled houses had their doors shut, spotless curtains shrouding their gleaming windows. From time to time they met a housewife, basket on arm, going to the shops, and exchanged good mornings, and they stopped frequently to look in the shop windows.

Eulalia found them fascinating—book shops galore and antiques shops, some with their goods spread out on the narrow pavement. Aderik bought her a small china bowl, patterned in the lavender colour, which was the first Delftware. It had a small chip and a hairline crack yet was none the less expensive, but since she didn't know the price and Mr van der Leurs paid without comment she accepted it with delight.

It was as they were on their way back, going down a narrow lane with a few shops and rather shabby cottages, that Eulalia stopped suddenly before a window. There was a kitten sitting in a cage there, a puny little creature with huge eyes. Attached to the cage was a card with '*Goedkoop*' written on it.

Eulalia tugged at Aderik's sleeve. 'How could anyone be so callous?' she demanded. 'Writing ''cheap'' on that card, just as though the little creature is fit for nothing. And supposing no one wants him? He'll just die.'

Mr van der Leurs looked down at her furious face, flushed with rage, her eyes flashing. She looked so beautiful he could hardly keep his hands off her. He said, 'We want him; he's just the companion Humbert will enjoy.'

The smile she gave him was his reward. 'You'll buy him? I'll look after him; he won't be a nuisance...'

He opened the door and its old-fashioned bell tinkled rustily and an elderly man came through the curtain at the back of the shop. Eulalia couldn't understand what was said; the man sounded apologetic and had a great deal to say while Aderik listened silently. Presently he handed the man some notes and the kitten was fetched out from the window, removed from his cage and transferred to the inside of Aderik's topcoat, and they were ushered out of the shop with some ceremony.

'Oh, Aderik, thank you. I'm sure he'll grow into a splendid cat. That horrible man...'

'He had a so-called pet shop there but is moving away. He sold the animals he had, and the shop, but this small creature for some reason wasn't sold, so he put it in the window as a last hope before being drowned.'

He added, 'Don't be sad; he's going to be our family pet and he's too small to remember his unhappy start. We'll cut through here; there's a shop in the next street where we can buy him a basket and anything else he needs.'

Eulalia was struggling not to cry. She had no reason to do so; the kitten was safe, Aderik had dealt with the unhappy little episode with instant calm; for some reason she realised that was why she wanted to cry. And that was absurd. He was a man of unfailing kindness. She might not know him very well yet but of that she was sure. And she trusted him...

Back at the house the kitten was laid on a clean towel, given warm milk and gently examined. He was in poor shape but Aderik thought that with good food and tender loving care he had a good chance of growing into a handsome cat. All the same, he would take him to the vet when he got home later in the day. So the kitten was settled in the basket Aderik had bought for him, lined with paper and a blanket, before the warm hearth. Humbert, at first doubtful and puzzled, came and sat beside him and presently, to their delight, the kitten crawled out of his basket and curled up between Humbert's paws.

Mr van der Leurs was late home; the bone marrow transplant he had done that afternoon had had unexpected complications and he would have to go back to the hospital later on. Nevertheless he took the kitten to the vet before he sat down to his dinner.

'Nothing wrong with him,' he assured Eulalia.

'He's had his injections and a thorough overhaul; all he needs now is feeding up and warmth.'

'And to be loved,' said Eulalia. 'And he must have a name—an important one to make up for an unhappy start. Something grand...'

They were sitting in the drawing room with Humbert lying on Aderik's feet and the kitten half buried against the great dog's furry chest.

'Ferdinand,' said Eulalia, 'and we can call him Ferdie. Oh, Aderik, I'm so glad you saved him.'

'He's made himself at home; I hear that Katje is mincing chicken and keeping milk warm on the Aga and obviously Humbert is pleased to have him.'

He got up carefully from his chair. 'I have to go back to the hospital. I'll say goodnight, Lally, and see you at breakfast. Ko will see to Humbert and Ferdie.'

He brushed her cheek with a quick kiss, a brief salute which left her feeling lonely.

'How can I possibly feel lonely?' asked Lally of her two companions.

And indeed she had no leisure to feel lonely; the next day was spent attending to Ferdie's needs, taking Humbert for a walk and then getting down to the serious business of dressing for the ball. She had decided on the pink taffeta and when she was finally dressed she had to admit that she really looked rather nice. She had taken pains with her face and her hair, and the fine cashmere shawl which she had had the forethought to buy made a warm and dramatic wrap against the cold night. There remained nothing for her to do but go down to the drawing room and wait for Aderik.

He was late, she thought worriedly; perhaps there had been an emergency which would hold him up for hours, and they might have to miss the first part of the evening, even the whole evening. She sat there trying not to fidget in case it creased her dress, thinking how much she had been looking forward to the ball. She hadn't been to a dance for a long time; she had always refused invitations to the annual dance at St Chad's; she couldn't afford a dress for one thing and for another she had been afraid that no one would dance with the canteen lady... But now she had the right clothes and a husband to partner her, and she very much wanted to dance with Aderik.

She glanced at the clock once more, heard voices in the hall and just had time to compose her features into serenity as the door opened and Aderik came in.

Annoyingly unhurried. Eulalia bit back wifely admonishments to hurry up and change, smiled as though time were of no importance at all, and said, 'Hello, Aderik. Would you like a drink before you change?'

He had shut the door and was leaning against it looking at her.

'Eulalia, you leave me speechless. I was prepared to see an impatient virago hissing at me to hurry up and change and did I know the time?

Instead of which I find a charming vision in pink offering me a drink!'

He crossed the room and pulled her to her feet. 'You look beautiful and that is a most becoming gown.' He held her away so that he could study her at his leisure. 'My enchanting wife,' he said quietly and then dropped her hands and added briskly, 'Give me fifteen minutes,' and was gone...

He was as good as his word and returned the epitome of a well-dressed man with time on his hands.

Eulalia said uncertainly, 'You won't leave me alone, will you?'

He hid a smile. 'No, Lally, although I think that you will have more partners than you will be able to cope with. Shall we go?' When she got up and picked up her wrap, he added, 'Just a moment,' and took a long box from an inner pocket. 'I have never given you a wedding present, have I?'

He took the double row of pearls from the box and fastened it round her neck and bent to kiss her. 'I wanted you to feel free, Lally...'

She knew what he meant; he had wanted her to marry him without any strings attached. She said simply, 'Thank you, Aderik. You are so good to me and thank you for that too.'

She turned to look in the gilt wood mirror above a wall table and put a hand up to touch the pearls. 'They're very beautiful.'

The ball was being held in the assembly hall of the hospital and the place was packed. The ter Brandts were standing by the doors, shaking hands and exchanging greetings as the guests arrived. Christina kissed Eulalia and said warmly, 'You look lovely; Aderik must be so proud of you. He'll be lucky to have more than two or three dances with you. Daisy and Jules are here already; it's quite a crush but you'll find them when the dancing stops.'

She turned to Aderik and Duert kissed Eulalia's cheek. 'I shall want a dance with you later,' he told her.

They joined the dancers then—they were playing a waltz and she gave herself up to the delight of dancing; it was as though she and Aderik had danced together all their lives and for a moment she was oblivious of anything but his arm around her and her feet following his of

their own volition. But presently he said, 'There are many people here whom you met when you came to see St Nikolaas, but you won't remember all of them.'

He was greeting other couples as they danced and she hastened to nod and smile too, feeling shy. When the dance ended and a rather pompous man and his wife approached them, Aderik said, 'You remember Professor Keesman, Eulalia? And his wife?'

Eulalia murmured politely and Mevrouw Keesman said kindly, 'You have met so many new faces, it must be difficult for you. You must come and visit me soon— after Christmas perhaps? I should like that.'

Eulalia barely had time to thank her before Professor Keesman danced her off into a slow foxtrot. He was a short stout man and she discovered quickly that he was self-important too, impressing upon her the high rank of his position in the hospital. She listened politely, making appropriate replies when necessary, thinking that Aderik never boasted about his work, nor did Duert, and she suspected that they were just as important as the professor. She hoped that Aderik wasn't a close friend of the Kessmans; she much preferred Duert and Jules.

But if she didn't much care for the professor there were any number of guests there who professed to be close friends of Aderik. She didn't lack for partners and from time to time she would find him at her elbow introducing her to one or other of them and claiming her for a dance.

They had supper with Daisy and Jules and half a dozen couples who obviously knew each other well and Eulalia got up from the supper table with enough invitations to fill her days for weeks to come. And when they went back into the ballroom Aderik whisked her onto the dance floor.

'Now we can dance together until the end,' he told her. 'My duty dances are done and you have had partners tumbling over each other to get at you; now we can behave like an old married couple and dance together.'

'Oh, yes, please,' said Eulalia. 'I feel so comfortable with you and I've run out of polite small talk!'

'But you are enjoying yourself? You have been much admired.'

'I've had a lovely time. I did my best to behave like a consultant's wife. I hope I didn't let you down. I mean, not remembering names and not being amusing or witty.'

She felt his arm tightening round her. 'My dear Eulalia, do not, I beg you, try to change in any way. You are delightful as you are, restful and soft-voiced and with the happy knack of knowing when to talk and when to keep silent.'

In other words, reflected Eulalia, dull. It was a depressing thought but if that was what he wanted in a wife then she would endeavour to be just that.

> **CHRISTMAS TIP**
> If you've got a large gift to wrap, try using a paper tablecloth. At this time of year you can usually find something suitably festive.

Somehow—she wasn't sure why—the pleasures and the excitement of the evening had evaporated. Which was absurd. She had had partners and compliments and there had been young women of her own age only too ready to make friends.

She watched Daisy and Jules dancing together and had a sudden pang of envy. And the ter Brandts, no longer in their first youth but obviously devoted... But of course they're in love, thought Eulalia wistfully.

The ball wound to a close and the guests began a leisurely departure, calling goodnights, stopping to chat with friends before going out into the cold night.

Back home, Aderik said, 'Shall we have a warm drink before we go to bed? Katje will have left something ready for us.'

The kitchen was cosy and neither Humbert nor Ferdie did more than open an eye as they went in.

'Hot cocoa?' suggested Eulalia, and

fetched mugs from the dresser and the plate of sandwiches she had asked Katje to make. 'Supper seems a long while ago,' she observed. 'I asked Katje to make them with ham and there's cold chicken...'

'Bless you for being a thoughtful housewife,' said Aderik, and took a huge mouthful before sitting down at the table opposite her. 'What a pleasant way to end the evening.'

He smiled at her. 'And you looked lovely, Lally. I am a very much envied man.'

She thanked him gravely. 'I've never been to a grand ball before; it was exciting.' She put down her mug. 'I think I'll go to bed.'

He got up and went to the door with her. 'Shall we go and buy the Christmas tree in the morning? I've private patients to see in the afternoon but otherwise I'm free.'

'Oh, yes—and a little one for Katje and Ko and Mekke?'

'Of course. We'll go into the country. Goodnight, Lally.'

She went to her bed feeling deprived. A good-night kiss would have set the seal on the evening.

It was mid-morning before they set out. Humbert had to have his walk, Ferdie needed to be fed and brushed and made much of and Katje needed to discuss what they should have for dinner that evening...

'We'll have lunch out,' said Aderik. 'I need to be back soon after one o'clock.'

He drove out of Amsterdam and took the road to Hilversum, some twenty miles away, and then turned off the main road into a narrow country lane running between flat fields. There was wooded country ahead of them and when they reached it there was a small village, well hidden from the road.

Aderik parked by a small farm at the edge of the village and they got out and walked across the yard and round the back to find an old man surrounded by Christmas trees in all shapes and sizes. He shouted a greeting to Mr van der Leurs and came to shake hands and then shake Eulalia's. He had a great deal to say, too, in his gruff old voice, nodding and shaking his head and then leading them among the trees. They chose a splendid one for the house and a small one for the kitchen and Eulalia wandered off, leaving Aderik to pay and talk to the man. Presently he joined her.

'The trees will be delivered in two days' time. They'll be in tubs and his son will bring them and carry them into the house.'

'He'll need a tip? How much do I give him?'

'Ten guilden—I've paid for transport...'

'And a cup of coffee,' said Eulalia, very much the housewife.

Christmas was near now; Eulalia's days

were filled wrapping presents, deciding on menus with Katje—a hilarious business with Ko patiently translating the more complicated remarks, although he was quick to tell her that her Dutch was improving each day. And then there was Humbert needing a walk even on a wet day, and Ferdie, still puny but beginning to look more like a kitten should.

There was Daisy to visit too and new-found friends phoning and Christina coming for coffee. Life was perfect, Eulalia told herself, ignoring the thought that all the same there was something not quite right... Perhaps it was because she didn't see much of Aderik: an hour or two in the evening, a brief half-hour at breakfast.

It was Christina who told her that he had agreed to take several teaching rounds. 'And I can't think why,' she added. 'Duert told him that they could be fitted in after the New Year so that he could be free instead of staying at the hospital in the afternoons.' She didn't say any more because she had seen the look on Eulalia's face. Had they quarrelled? she wondered, and dismissed the idea as absurd, sorry that she had said it.

Eulalia tried to forget about it. Aderik had his reasons for wanting to fill his days with work and when he was home he was as kind and friendly to her as he always was—only he was so seldom home...

She told herself she was worrying about nothing and flung herself into the final

arrangements for the arrival of their guests.

Paul arrived first on the day before Christmas Eve, breezing into the house just before lunch, clapping Ko on the back, kissing Katje and Mekke, hugging Eulalia, demanding to know where Aderik was. He was almost as tall as his brother and very like him in looks, bubbling over with good spirits.

'I'm not supposed to be here until this evening, am I? But I couldn't wait to meet you. You're even more beautiful than Aderik said. Am I in my usual room? Is lunch at half-past twelve? I'm famished.'

Eulalia liked him. When he was ten years older he would be just like Aderik.

'How much longer will you be in Leiden?' she asked over lunch.

'Another year. I'm qualified but I want to specialise. I'd like to go to England, work in a hospital there and get some experience. Of course I'll never reach the heights Aderik has—he's top of the tree. I only hope I'll be half as good.'

They took Humbert for his walk presently and soon after they got back Aderik came home in time to greet the rest of his family, his arm around Eulalia as he introduced her to his mother who was unexpectedly small and plump with grey hair pulled severely back from a kind face, to his sisters, tall and good-looking, and their husbands and five children.

'It is too bad,' said Mevrouw van der Leurs, 'that you should have to meet all of us at once, and more so since Aderik tells me that you have no family. But we welcome you most warmly, Eulalia, and hope that you will adopt us as your own.' Eulalia, hugged and kissed and made much of, reflected that this was going to be a wonderful Christmas.

> ### DID YOU KNOW?
> The tradition of eating mince pies dates back to the 16th century. It follows the belief that for every day of the twelve days of Christmas that you eat a mince pie you will have a happy month to follow.

And so it was. The children were small enough to believe in Father Christmas and the old house rang with their small voices, and after tea everyone helped decorate the tree, glittering with baubles and with a magnificent fairy doll topping it, and then they all went to the kitchen while Katje and Ko decorated the smaller tree with the children's help.

Since it was Christmas time dinner was served earlier than usual so that the children could stay up for it, and Eulalia, looking round the table, thought how marvellous it was to belong to such a happy family. She caught Aderik's eye, sitting at the head of the table, and beamed at him, and he smiled back briefly as he turned to speak to his mother.

For a moment she felt chilled. But it was impossible to be downcast; Paul took all her attention and when they got up from the table she went upstairs with Lucia and Marijka and helped them put the children to bed. Afterwards they sat and talked over coffee and the delicious little biscuits Katje had made.

Mevrouw van der Leurs declared that she was tired and would go to bed—the signal for everyone else to do the same. Eulalia, kissed goodnight and complimented on the delicious dinner and pleasant evening, was left alone with Aderik, and she asked anxiously, 'Was it really all right? Just as you wanted it?'

'It was perfect, Eulalia.'

'Oh, good. Your mother is a darling, isn't she? And your sisters and brother and the children.' She gave a small sigh. 'They're all so happy.'

'Does that mean that you're not, Lally?'

'No, no, of course not. I was only thinking that I've missed so much. Although Grandfather and Jane were always so good to me.' She added sharply, 'I'm not whinging...'

'No, no; I never thought you were. I'm glad that you do like the family—your family as well as mine.'

'Well, I think it's very nice of them not to mind that you married me in such a hurry.' She got up. 'I'm going to bed. Will you make sure that Ferdie's comfortable when you take Humbert to his basket?'

He went to open the door for her. 'I'm going to the hospital in the morning but I'll be back for lunch. Would you like to go to the midnight service at the English church?'

'Oh, yes. Daisy told me about it. All of us?'

'No, just you and me. The family will go to morning service which will give us the chance to put the presents round the tree.'

Her eyes shone. 'It's like a fairy-tale Christmas,' she told him, and leaned up to kiss his cheek.

Mr van der Leurs went back to his chair. In fairy tales, he reflected, the prince always won the hand of the princess. Which was what he intended to do.

Christmas Eve passed in a happy bustle: last-minute talks with Katje, walking with Paul and the children and Humbert while Lucia and Marijka saw to the children's presents, Ferdie to feed and play with, chatting to her mother-in-law over coffee and then Aderik coming home and the house alive with children's voices. But all five had an early supper and were put to bed and dinner was a leisurely meal with easy talk and a lot of laughter.

The house was quiet when Aderik and Eulalia went out to the car. It was bitterly cold but there were stars and half a moon casting its icy light. The city was thronged with people and although the shops were long since shut their lighted windows rivalled the lighted Christmas trees in the squares. The church was in a small enclosure off Kalverstraat, surrounded by a ring of old houses, and was already almost full. Eulalia saw Christina and Duert ter Brandt almost at once, and then Daisy and Jules.

There was a Christmas tree and holly and flowers and a choir. It was all so English and she felt tears prick her eyelids. The congregation burst into the opening carol and after a moment she joined in.

It took some time to leave the church once the service was over, there were so many people to exchange good wishes with. The streets were quieter now and the shop windows dark, but as they reached the house she could see a glimmer of light through the transom over the door and inside it was warm and very welcoming.

'Coffee in the kitchen if you would like it,' she told Aderik, and went ahead of him to fill the mugs and get it ready.

He came into the kitchen presently, took the mugs from her and set them on the table. 'Happy Christmas, Lally. I'm cheating and giving you your present while we are alone together.'

It was earrings, gold and diamonds with a pearl drop.

Eulalia looked up at him. 'Aderik—they

are so very beautiful; I've never seen anything as lovely. Thank you over and over again; you are so good and kind to me.' She kissed his cheek. 'May I try them on now?'

She slipped the hooks into her ears and went to look in the small looking-glass by the dresser, turning this way and that, her eyes shining.

It would be so easy, he thought, watching her, to play on her happiness and gratitude, but that wasn't what he wanted. If she came to love him it had to be of her own free will...

'Could I wear them to breakfast?'

He laughed then. 'Well, perhaps lunch would be a better choice. What dress are you wearing?'

'The russet velvet you chose.' She beamed at him as she sat down to drink her coffee. 'I'm so happy I could burst,' she told him, and presently, her coffee drunk, she wished him goodnight and went off to bed, still wearing the earrings.

Everyone was up early in the morning and breakfast was eaten to a chorus of seasonal greetings. The children could hardly eat for excitement and were presently borne away to church, leaving Aderik and Eulalia to collect up the presents and arrange them round the tree.

They went to the kitchen first with the gifts for Katje, Ko and Mekke. Wim was there too, shaking hands and having a great deal to say to Eulalia, who didn't understand a word but made up for that by smiling a lot and looking interested. He was profuse in his thanks for the box of cigars and the envelope Mr van der Leurs gave him and went to sit by the Aga, for he was to spend the day there, joining in the festivities.

The presents arranged, Aderik took Humbert for his walk and Eulalia fetched Ferdie to sit in his little basket in the drawing room and then everyone was back from church to drink coffee.

Eulalia had decided that their traditional Christmas dinner should be eaten at midday so that the children could join in before the presents were handed out. She had taken great pains with the table and on her way upstairs went to check that everything was just so. It looked magnificent with the white damask cloth, silver and sparkling glass. She had made a centrepiece with holly and Christmas roses and gold ribbon and the napkins were tied with red ribbon. She went to her room then, got into the russet velvet dress and fastened the pearls, put in the earrings and went back to the drawing room.

That night curled up in her bed, waiting for sleep, Eulalia re-lived the day. It was one that she would always remember for it had been perfect. Christmas dinner had been a success; the turkey, the Christmas pudding, the mince pies, the wines and champagne had all been praised. And as for the presents, everyone had declared that everything they had received was exactly what they wanted.

She closed her eyes to shut out the thought that she and Aderik had had no time to be together, had exchanged barely a dozen words. If she hadn't been so sleepy she might have worried about that.

In Holland, she had discovered, there wasn't a Boxing Day but a second Christmas Day, only the names were different. The day was spent looking at presents again, going for a walk, playing games with the children and having friends in for drinks in the evening. She spent it being a good hostess, making endless light conversation with Aderik's friends and their wives, trying out her fragmented Dutch on her sisters-in-law, being gently teased by Paul and all the while wishing for Aderik's company.

Everyone went home the next day and the house was suddenly quiet, for Aderik had gone to the hospital in the early morning. She had slipped down to sit with him while he had breakfast but there was no time for a leisurely talk.

'I shall probably be late home,' he'd told her, getting up to leave. 'I've a list this morning and a clinic in the afternoon.'

She mooned around the house with Humbert padding beside her and Ferdie tucked under one arm. 'I do miss them all,'

she told Humbert, and then changed that to, 'I do miss Aderik.'

It was nearly lunchtime when Ko came looking for her. He looked so anxious that she said, 'Ko, what's the matter? Are you ill?'

'*Mevrouw*, there has been a message from the hospital, from the director. There has been an explosion in one of the theatres and I am to tell you not to worry.'

'Aderik,' said Eulalia—and, thrusting Ferdie at Ko, flew past him and into the hall, to drag on an elderly mac she kept for the garden. She dashed out of the house, racing along the narrow streets, oblivious of the cold rain and the slippery cobbles. If he's hurt, I'll die, she told herself. She said loudly, 'Oh, Aderik, I love you. I think I always have and now perhaps it's too late and how silly of me not to know.'

She glared at a solitary woman standing in her way and pushed past her. She was sopping wet and bedraggled when she reached the hospital and the porter on duty gave her a shocked look and started towards her, but she flew past him and belted up the stairs to the theatre unit. She had to pause then for the place was thronged with firemen and police and porters carrying away equipment. They were all too busy to notice her. She edged her way through, looking for someone who would know where Aderik was. He might even now be being treated for injuries—or worse, said a small voice in the back of her head.

She was dodging in and out of the various side rooms and then saw the main theatre at the end of the corridor, its doors off the hinges, everything in it twisted and smashed. She slithered to a halt and almost fell over when Aderik said from somewhere behind her, 'My dear, you shouldn't be here.'

She turned on him. 'Why didn't you tell me, phone me? You must have known I'd be half out of my mind. You could have been hurt—killed. I'm your wife.' She burst into tears. 'And it doesn't matter to you but I love you and I really will not go on like this.'

She stopped, aware that she was babbling, that that was the last thing she had meant to say to him. She wiped a hand across a tear-stained cheek and muttered, 'I didn't mean to say that.' She gave a great sniff and said in a small polite voice, 'I hope you haven't been hurt.'

Mr van der Leurs wasted a moment or so looking at her—hair in wet streamers, a tear-smeared face, in an old mac fit for the refuse bin and thin slippers squelching water. And so beautiful...!

He removed the wet garment from her and took her into his arms.

'My darling,' he said gently, 'why do you suppose I married you?'

'You wanted a wife.' She sniffed again.

'Indeed I did. You. I fell in love with you the moment I set eyes on you at St Chad's. I knew that you didn't love me, but I was sure that if I had patience you would find that you love me too.'

'You never said...' mumbled Eulalia.

'I cherished the thought that you would discover it without any help from me.'

His arms tightened around her. 'I'm going to kiss you,' he said.

'Oh, yes, please,' said Eulalia.

They stood there, the chaos around them forgotten, watched by silent onlookers: firemen, doctors, police and porters and the odd nurse, all of them enjoying the sight of two people in love. ■

To solve a **Hitori** puzzle, shade the squares so that the numbers only appear once in each column or row. Not every number needs to appear in each column or row... but remember, they cannot appear more than once! Shaded squares cannot be next to each other in a row or a column. Unshaded squares must be connected to another unshaded square either vertically or horizontally.

7	7	6	6	1	1	1	3
4	3	8	2	1	5	6	7
2	8	6	8	7	2	4	5
1	8	7	7	2	2	2	4
7	8	3	5	4	8	1	1
1	4	1	2	2	2	7	8
6	5	7	4	3	7	4	1
3	5	7	1	1	4	5	3

 Solutions on page 174 **87**

Horoscopes

Find out what 2007 holds for you! By Dadhichi Toth

AQUARIUS
21 January – 18 February

Romance and Friendship
As 2007 gets moving, your relationships demand extra attention. You need time to sift through issues *without* pressure. Your decisions must come from your heart, not your head.

In January and February, friends will make their demands known. Luckily Jupiter will give you the strength to smooth over these difficult moments. In April and May, Venus uplifts your prospects for romance. This is a time of wild love affairs. Be on guard against impulsive passion. You'll meet several people and your initial actions may cause regret afterwards. Throughout June and July, Venus triggers marriage issues. This could fulfil your dreams of a long-term relationship. Your love affairs and travel will coincide throughout November. This is a chance for you to step outside your normal routine and enjoy a little bit of socialising in a far-off place.

Career and Finances
Due to the strength of Mars at the outset of 2007, you'll be all fired up to make money. As February comes around, your lucky planet Venus gives you the chance to earn money from unexpected quarters. In March be careful that your drive to achieve goals doesn't put you offside with others. Lucky investments increase cash throughout June. Study your financial portfolio. If you have property, learn how to use your equity to work for you.
Secure that new job in November when the Sun boosts your career. A promotion brings you increased income.

Karma and Luck
Your luck is connected to your social life in 2007. Working with a social club at work or taking on a greater responsibility for the 'group' will inspire and add a new dimension to your life.

PISCES
19 February – 20 March

Romance and Friendship
2007 will be one of the most exciting love periods of your life. Your love affairs are particularly stimulating in February, April and May. Amorous opportunities will be dizzying.
During May you're dynamic, active and also passionate. Venus and Mercury in June stimulate

your creativity. Children feature strongly at this time too.

Emotional satisfaction in August will be scarce. Your heart desperately wants to improve relationships. There'll be opportunities to rekindle love though.

In October and November expect your love life to reach an all-time high. You have a chance to solidify a relationship. 2007 will certainly be full of rich emotional experiences.

Career and Finances

Throughout March, April and May, contracts will be signed to improve your finances. Venus triggers property matters. Question whether it's appropriate to invest further or dispose of existing property.

Profits will be up on July and you'll be able to plug any holes in the money 'bucket'. There's no point earning more if you're spending twice as much.

New partnerships are formed in August/ September, when your commercial interests reach a peak. Sudden twists in your schedule will work out to be a blessing

in disguise.

From September to December, your reputation will grow. Promotions and other opportunities present themselves. In 2007 your profession will be a source of great satisfaction.

Karma and Luck

Your lucky periods throughout 2007 are January, February and June. During these months get ready to attack your financial ambitions optimistically. With energy, initiative and fate all combining, these will be lucky months for you financially.

ARIES
21 March – 20 April

Romance and Friendship

2007 is an important year in which you'll meet those with shared romantic ideals. Your bright aura will attract social opportunities and potential soulmates. New romances will excite you as an inspiring love cycle begins.

Loads of fun and wonderful opportunities are available in February, April, June and July. Venus promises memorable and spicy encounters with lovers in these months. If you're already in a relationship, get ready for a revival of passion.

Superb moments of love will dazzle you in the latter part of the year when Venus moves to the most prominent part of your horoscope. Many of your activities will be strongly connected to love and sexuality.

Career and Finances

2007 will see Aries full of desire for leadership and recognition. You'll be increasing your professional efforts and determining your own destiny more powerfully than ever. As the year progresses, you'll move ahead in leaps and bounds.

This is a year for dynamic change in your career. Promotions result in better finances in January, March, April, July and November. Your efforts towards your goals are on target.

Karma and Luck

This is a brilliant year for all sorts of unexpected fortune. Aries' lucky planets, Mars and Jupiter are in great form and shower you with superior health. Your optimistic thinking will improve your wellbeing and luck generally. Expect some of your best fortune in years. Your zone of journeys is especially influenced by these lucky planets so take a long, relaxing trip and enjoy what Lady Luck has to offer.

TAURUS
21 April – 21 May

Romance and Friendship

Transformation is the keyword for your relationships in 2007. Lovers, friends and family will notice your change in character. Due to Jupiter in your zone of sexuality this makeover will affect the most intimate parts of your life. It will influence you all year.

Romantic opportunities present themselves in greater measure. This will happen in the most unusual ways due to Uranus. In April and May your passion and personal charisma will attract loads of attention. Sexual opportunities are great in February, March, June, July and August. Favourable planetary combinations excite you and in July marriage or at least long term commitments are focussed.

Career and Finances

Promotions and an improved professional standing will result in a better financial situation for you in 2007.

During March and April, your finance planets will create new economic opportunities. But there's also a danger of being lax in the way you manage your financial affairs. Be frugal! Investments are more profitable after Venus enters your speculative zone in August. At that time Jupiter, the planet of fortune, gives a decent boost to your cash flow.

Karma and Luck

You need to make a break and move forward independently. Your luck will only be inhibited by your reliance on others. Promote a freer and independent lifestyle so your fortune will increase. Cultural and artistic interests need to be developed in 2007. Educate yourself in art, music and literature. This will work like a dream for you and open your heart to new possibilities.

GEMINI
22 May – 22 June

Romance and Friendship

Prepare for some extraordinary romantic highlights during 2007! People will feel inspired by your positive and upbeat energy. This will attract new lovers to you. Sudden events occur in February, when Venus connects with exciting Uranus. After March your committed relationships will see a sobering influence.

In early May unusual meetings cause you to reconsider your relationships. Your one-on-one affairs will be much more activated during September when Mars and Jupiter fully influence your marital sector.

In November Jupiter edges closer to its rendezvous with the

deep and mysterious Pluto. This is an important month to consolidate the gains in your relationships.

Career and Finances

Mars dominates your profession in 2007. Its connection with Jupiter is an excellent omen for your work and professional destiny. Promotions and other opportunities for increased prestige take place in February. Uranus continues to influence your professional affairs generally throughout the whole year. The new Moon of the 17th April brings a fatter pay cheque and fresh work opportunities.

One of the better months of the year is October as shown by the full Moon in your profit sector. Those long-awaited bonuses or owed money might finally surface and bring a smile to your face.

Karma and Luck

Sharing your talents will by far be the best way in which you can increase your fortune in 2007. Because work is the arena in which most of these influences will be felt, you can expect great luck in this specific

department of your life.

CANCER
23 June – 22 July

Romance and Friendship

Friendship, companionship and a more popular period are characterised by 2007. In January you'll feel a transformative influence as Venus touches your most personal affairs.

Mars causes heat in February. Issues of control will be dealt with. You have a strong urge to take action, not just talk. You must be careful not to allow your emotions to get the better of you.

In April and May expect trying incidents with your friends. Ego issues come to a head. Your loyalty will be tested as you balance your own self interests and devotion to others. In September tackle communication concerns. Stubborn people will have to contend with you. Domestic affairs undergo immense changes. In December your enjoyment of children is highlighted. You'll

enjoy improved relations with kids.

Career and Finances

You'll spend the first part of 2007 planning your strategies with tremendous energy and charisma. You can combine these forces to achieve your goals in 2007.

During May and June social activities are a relief from the intense workload earlier in the year. Journeys in July will recharge your weary nerves. Travel with friends is on the cards. In September, look forward to solidifying deals on the table. There's a chance to formalise an agreement.

The Sun offers extremely good monetary results in April, August and December. Enjoy the year, as it is likely to be successful financially.

Karma and Luck

Venus is lucky for you and shows that your relationships in 2007 are likely to be a source of great happiness and successful introductions. Allocate enough time to further develop your levels of intimacy.

LEO

23 July – 23 August

Romance and Friendship
In 2007 love is probably
more important for Leo
than any other star sign.
Jupiter, Mars and Pluto in
your romance sector
mean love and romance
is on your mind
this year. Throughout
January and February
you'll be meeting new
people at work and
forging new love affairs.
Feel free to develop
these associations,
bearing in mind the
consequences of
workplace romances.
There's a strong focus on
marriage during the
months of March, July
and December and this
also relates to friends and
relatives getting married
or engaged.
Venus moves to your
domestic sphere in
December. You'll prefer
quiet time with your lover
in a secluded
environment. As much as
you'd prefer your own
company you'll be with
lots of new friends at
Christmas time.

Career and Finances
Banking and insurance
matters are scrutinised
throughout February and
need a watchful eye.
Don't waste your money
by taking the first offer.
March and April are
legally orientated with
extra paperwork
spotlighted. Good
income, especially in
May, is forecast.
Throughout June and July
you're able to secure a
much coveted job. From
August you're
invigorated. Your
competitive urges will be
strong and you can
achieve a lot.
September, October and
November are strong
months for extra bonuses.
If you run an
independent business, it's
also great for increased
sales.

Karma and Luck
Theatre, music and other
artistic activities are likely
to be lucky romantically.
Your creative energies
are revved up by cultural
pursuits. Networking with
others creates fortunate
breaks for you.

VIRGO

24 August – 22 September

Romance and Friendship
Throughout 2007 your
social life brings you to a
new level of awareness.
In February sexual
encounters give you a
whole new sense of self
worth.
In April when Venus
moves through your work
zone, your social life
could take a dramatic
turn as work colleagues
double as lovers.
During May new
relationships formed result
in marriage or de facto
situations. If you're single
this could be what
you've been waiting for.
From July you radiate
great charisma. You'll be
changing your overall
fashion statement,
hairstyles and makeup
as well.
In November and
December open
discussions with friends.
You'll finally decide
whom you're going to
keep in your life.

Career and Finances

Your finances are highly speculative in 2007. You're not afraid to take a punt and try new things.

January, February and March are strong professionally. A new job comes your way. Your day-to-day routine will change but sudden financial glitches cause setbacks.

Good profits are likely in June when Venus presents you windows of opportunity which are too good to refuse.

In December an unexpected windfall could be a wonderful conclusion to the year. It's best to keep this to yourself, as it will be pretty easy for you to share (waste?) your winnings with others.

Karma and Luck

In March and April lucky transits bring travel. Adventure will top your list giving you the chance to meet many new people. Your interest in alternative philosophy will be underlined this year. You're due for a positive return on your karma throughout 2007 so enjoy the ride.

LIBRA

23 September – 23 October

Romance and Friendship

You have a strong attraction to traditional romance this year. This means friendship with practical and conventional characters. Your social life also attracts you to wealthy, powerful people.

Your romance connects you with creative people. Expect plenty of fun times, especially in February and March when love coincides with entertainment.

Between July and September Venus causes unusual romances. This can be unsettling if you're not prepared for uncommon friendships. Expect dazzling communications in November/December, when Mercury and Venus activate you. You'll make exceptional headway using humour in your social interaction.

All in all, 2007 is a positive turning point for most Librans. Balance your dreams with the practical requirements of romance.

Career and Finances

You feel practical this year. Traditional forms of investment will be beneficial. You'll be a magnet for extra pay rises during April, May and July.

Starting new courses of study will be excellent during June. Get your books and paperwork out for that mid-year course.

Restrictions are relieved when Saturn exits your sector of profits, bolstering earnings. This is enhanced by September. In October Venus connects you with important people to give you a financial edge.

2007 is a year of achievement, ingenuity and exciting new opportunities.

Karma and Luck

Mercury, a very lucky planet for you, brings you fortune in your family affairs this year. This is also an excellent period to consider a long-term commitment with someone you're friends with or have known for a while.

Your luck planets ensure a happy journey throughout 2007.

SCORPIO
24 October – 22 November

Romance and Friendship
2007 is a most magical time and will bring out the best of luck and fortune for you. You are giving off powerful signals and the Universe will respond.

Venus activates your romance zone in February and March. Use your charm. It makes you seductive and popular. You'll meet long-lost lovers and feel a rekindling of past feelings.

In April and May Venus will nudge you in the area of marriage and sex. You're likely to do something dramatically impulsive. Use your better judgement.

Venus comes to your friendship zone in November. It's time to renew friendships and seek out new contacts which fulfil you.

2007 will be a special year to be remembered and love, in particular, will bring you many exciting memories for the future.

Career and Finances
It seems that work changes take effect from March and April when Venus affects your employment. You'll transform your career and make good impressions on others. You can shine like the Sun so vigour and ambition is renewed.

In July more scrutiny and legal advice for an informed decision are necessary. Crossing all your T's and dotting all your I's will pay handsome dividends throughout August and September. Minor setbacks in September are temporary, so enjoy the financial rewards.

Karma and Luck
Lucky breaks are startling in 2007. You have a speculative mind and anything you touch will work in your favour. The odd lottery ticket or gamble will bring you lucky wins.

You'll be surprised to receive unexpected windfalls, wills and other lump sums. Don't blow it all, Scorpio.

SAGITTARIUS
23 November – 21 December

Romance and Friendship
You're optimistic that in 2007 your relationships will have a new lease of life. You'll meet stacks of new people. Social variety and friendship are the keywords for 2007.

Initially your relationships will be dominated by financial matters and by February/March you'll find your romantic interest waning as you concentrate on family.

In May Venus makes you prone to bettering your partnerships. Issues with your partner will resolve. You will find your emotional and financial needs are somehow linked in June.

Expect greater vitality during the months of July and August when your self esteem will be at an all-time high.

Career and Finances
Venus in your finance zone early in 2007 is a great boost for your financial and professional life. Saturn will cause you to rethink many of your

professional objectives though.

You'll be tested in August when the Sun prods your work responsibilities. Health and vitality will be increasingly vital to your success. Diarising your plans will be essential. September is an excellent month for your star sign and you can expect your efforts to be crowned with success. You'll be recognised for your steady work.

November requires a watchful review of your banking and debt situation. Renewing contracts or accounts with your bank manager, accountant or legal advisers is not a bad manoeuvre.

Karma and Luck

Your financial luck is strong in January and April and incredibly high-powered in September and October. Don't let opportunities pass you by. Throughout June there are meetings which will offer unique opportunities. 2007 is one of your luckiest in twelve years so don't waste a moment.

CAPRICORN
22 December – 20 January

Romance and Friendship

Romantic burdens in February/March must be looked at rationally. Don't take out your frustrations on loved ones.

Throughout March family life is enhanced. April is an excellent month to foster your romantic interests.

June offers a wonderful cycle for deepening the bonds of love and tying the knot. If you're unattached, share the joy of Venus' blessings.

Venus moves through your sexual zone in July, the zone of travels in August and the arena of sexuality in September. These months are important for going over old ground in order to understand your relationships.

If you've been inhibited, new ground can be broken in August. Throughout October you'll be confounded by a new person entering your life who's magnetic and totally youthful.

Career & Finances

Take your work home in March and April if you must, but talk yourself out of being a workaholic even though you'll get more done.

In June expect conflict with those calling the shots. You'll have strong ideas about your work but will be up against a brick wall convincing others.

In June and July business partnerships emerge. You can attract money for independent plans. Cut a deal for change.

Manage your health and vitality well in August and September. In October stake your claim for a coveted position. There'll be surplus cash at this time.

Celebrations are in order in November, when you congratulate yourself on a job well done.

Karma & Luck

Luck will have to do with your personal appearance this year. Grooming yourself will be the key in attracting good fortune in 2007. ■

dating in the dark
Barbara Hannay

When the lift stopped and the lights went out, Jess panicked.

She knew she was about to die, horribly. She was going to crash twenty floors to her death – and she couldn't hold back a pathetic whimper.

"Don't worry." A man's voice came out of the darkness. "It's probably just a black-out."

"But I'm claustrophobic." She had flattened herself against the wall like a fridge magnet, as if, somehow, that would save her from falling to her doom.

"I'm sure we'll be OK. I read somewhere these things are counterbalanced."

Jess had no idea what that meant but it sounded reassuring and she was grateful.

She wished she'd taken more notice of her companion. Normally she checked out other people travelling in a lift with her. But today she'd backed into this lift talking on her mobile and balancing takeaway coffee. She'd pressed the button for her floor, only vaguely noticing a tall man in the corner.

A small glow appeared in the dark beside her. Her companion was using a mobile phone. Good idea. Why hadn't she thought of that? Hastily she retrieved hers from her handbag and dialled Carrie in the office.

The number was engaged. Carrie was notorious for gossiping with friends.

"The whole building's blacked out," announced the stranger as he snapped his phone shut. "Must be our lucky day."

"Oh, sure," said Jess. "Instead of crashing we can now slowly die from suffocation."

Already she was having trouble breathing. The walls of the lift were closing in on her. The thick blackness was oppressive, filling her nostrils and mouth. She tried to breathe deeply, but all she managed were frantic gasps.

"Are you OK?" His voice was very deep and pleasant with no hint of panic.

"No, I'm not OK." Jess knew she sounded pathetically scared, but she couldn't help it.

"We're not going to drop. There are all sorts of safety features in modern lifts."

"But it's so dark in here. It's really getting to me."

"Why don't you sit down?"

"All right." She slid her back down the wall till she reached the floor, set the coffee beside her and sat with her hands clasped tightly around her knees.

In the darkness she sensed her companion sitting, too. She had the impression of very long legs stretched out on the floor beside her.

"I'm supposed to be having an interview at nine o'clock," he said conversationally.

"A job interview?"

There was a short pause. "Yes," he said.

"Well, at least you have a good excuse for being late." She was pleased that her voice sounded less terrified and breathless now. "My name's Jess, by the way."

"Daniel," he said. His hand brushed her knee and she jumped. "I thought we should shake hands."

"Oh. Right."

In the dark, their hands fumbled and then clasped. Daniel's handshake was strong without crushing her. Warm. Reassuring.

If this scene was in a movie, thought Jess, Daniel and I would have found ourselves in some kind of clinch already.

"What sort of job are you applying for?" she asked.

"Ah – public relations."

"I have interviews scheduled for this morning, too. But I'm on the other side of the desk. I interview clients for – my company."

"Which company do you work for?"

"We do – um – social work." She felt a little uncomfortable talking about what she really did while she was alone in the dark with a strange man. He might get the wrong idea.

"So you help families in trouble, the elderly – that sort of thing?"

She'd always been hopeless at lying. "Actually, I may as well tell you, it's a dating agency."

This was met by a disconcerting silence.

"It's a very reputable agency," she added defensively.

"I'm glad to hear it. So what do you do? Compile a kind of dossier for each client?"

"Yes. I write a physical description and conduct an interview and then transfer the info onto computer files. It's quite interesting. I really enjoy it."

When Daniel didn't respond, Jess said, "Do you mind if we talk? I feel so much better when I'm talking."

"Well, maybe you could interview me."

"Why? Are you looking for a date?"

"It could be a warm-up for my – er – job interview."

"The questions aren't related to work."

"Give it a go. I'll start by describing what I look like."

"Let me guess. Tall and dark?"

"And exceptionally good-looking."

Jess laughed. "Or exceptionally conceited."

"Ouch. There's no need for brutal honesty."

She could tell by his voice that he

was smiling.

"Then you'll believe me if I tell you I'm a blonde, tall and willowy..." Willowy could never be an accurate description of her, but now seemed as good a time as any to borrow it. "No," said Daniel.

"OK, scratch the tall, willowy bit."

"You're not blonde either. You have medium brown hair, brown eyes. You're single, of average height and I'd say you're – about – a size 10."

"For heaven's sake." Jess blushed. He had described her to a T.

"Do you mean to tell me my personal details are on a glow-in-the-dark chip on my forehead?"

He laughed. "It's built into a guy's DNA to notice these things. Oh, and you're exceptionally pretty."

From somewhere in the lift well above them came a thumping sound. Jess had been calming down, but now she was suddenly as nervous as ever as she pictured the small box they were in breaking loose and plummeting downwards.

"Keep talking," she said. "Please!"

"What sort of questions do you ask at these dating interviews?"

"Oh, things like ... what's your best feature? What's your idea of a romantic date? Can you dance?" A pause. "Can you dance?"

"Badly, but with enthusiasm. You must get some interesting answers."

"Sometimes, but a lot of people are predictable. The most popular romantic date is dinner and a film."

"What's wrong with dinner and a film?"

"It's not very imaginative, is it?"

"So what's your idea of an imaginative romantic date, Jess?"

"Hey, I'm the one asking the questions."

"Answer this one."

"Well, I'm not particularly original either – but I'd rather like a drive into the country and a picnic on a shady river bank."

"Ever been on a date like that?"

"No." And now was not the time to admit her personal date drought. But working for a dating agency, she had become extra fussy. There were lots of OK guys around, but she was looking for someone more than OK. She wanted serious sparks.

"Your turn, Daniel. What's your idea of a romantic date?"

"Hard to know. I reckon the person you're with makes a date romantic. I mean, a guy could take a woman to a classy restaurant. Fly her to Paris for that matter, or Venice. It would be a hell of a romantic gesture, but it might also be a romantic flop."

"I doubt it."

"But don't you think that if you really fancy someone you could eat corned beef sandwiches or spend Saturday morning wandering around the supermarket and find it romantic?"

"Oh," Jess said softly, "yes, I do."

She felt unaccountably sad all of a sudden. She'd thought how wonderful it would be to be swept away by love, and for a second or two, while Daniel was talking she felt a leap inside her, like the spurt of a flame. But it was crazy to feel romantic about being trapped in a lift with him, just because he had a gorgeous voice.

"Then again," said Daniel. "It's rather romantic to be stuck in a lift with a pretty girl, too."

Jess felt another tide of heat flood her face and she was very grateful for the dark. "A kind of a blind date," she said.

Then the lights came on.

Jess blinked and her eyes met Daniel's. He smiled.

Jess smiled back. He had blue eyes and the nicest face. Hunky body, too. His appearance matched his voice. Perfectly. In that instant he was perfect.

The lift lurched and then began to climb slowly upwards. Jess clambered to her feet. They were stopping at Level twenty-five, her floor.

The doors slid open and she smiled. "Thank you for your company. You saved me from making a hysterical fool of myself."

"It was my pleasure. It was nice to meet you, Jess." His delightfully old-fashioned charm took her breath away.

"I hope you get the job," she said.

"Thanks."

She drifted into the office in a kind of miserable daze. Carrie was concerned and made her fresh coffee. "At least there was no one waiting here for an interview," she said. "The first client is probably still in the lobby waiting for the lift."

Jess glanced at the bookings. The first interview was with... Daniel Murray.

Daniel?

It had to be a coincidence. Quickly she checked his application form and the small passport sized photo.

Oh, no!

It was him. Her Daniel...from the lift.

Had he been too embarrassed to tell her the truth? Had their conversation put him off?

His mobile phone number was there on the form. She would have to ring him, otherwise she'd be a mess for the rest of the day. Then her phone rang.

"Jess, it's Daniel. From the lift."

Her hello was a nervous squeak. "I was about to phone you."

"Sorry about the job interview story. I'm normally straighter than that. But as you must have guessed, I've changed my mind."

In all honesty she couldn't imagine why Daniel would need the services of a dating agency. "Do you mind if I ask why you booked to come in?"

"It seemed like a good idea. I've recently moved to the city. I've tried bars and nightclubs, but city girls are so full on. They don't give a bloke room to manoeuvre."

Jess had a sudden picture of Daniel in a city nightclub fighting off girls and felt an irrational wave of jealousy.

"I'm sure you'll adjust pretty quickly."

"Perhaps, but I think I've come up with a more creative alternative."

"What's that?"

"I thought I'd jump in the deep-end and ask this really lovely girl I met if she'd fancy a drive in the country next weekend. Maybe a picnic on a shady river bank."

Jess's heart sang. "I'd say it's worth a try. So you're stealing my idea of an ideal date?"

"Would you be interested, Jess?"

With commendable decorum, she said, "What would you like me to bring?"

"I'll take care of the catering, if you don't mind simple fare. I understand that if two people really click, even corned beef sandwiches can be romantic."

She was grinning from ear to ear. "Corned beef sandwiches would be fabulous."

For a story packed with pure romance & pure emotion – look out for Claiming the Cattleman's Heart – by BARBARA HANNAY. Out in December in Mills & Boon Romance!

tired of turkey! ...

Well, turkey is traditional, isn't it?... There's much to recommend it – it's great at feeding large numbers of people, it's comforting, doesn't overwhelm all those yummy accompaniments. But not everyone loves it, and sometimes, well, it's just good to have a change.

For the last few years I've tested many Christmas recipes which are fresh and stimulating, can feed small or large amounts of people, yet bring to the table lots of those Christmassy tastes, textures and aromas that we just wouldn't want to live without. There are lots of fabulous alternatives, many of them quicker and easier to prepare and cook than a supersized turkey. The first time I cooked this beef dish my partner and I were spending Christmas cruising on a narrow boat up the Shropshire Union canal. I cooked it in the galley – basic though with a full-sized oven, as the frost-covered English countryside slowly passed by (and my partner did all the hard stuff – like opening locks and steering the boat)!

The beef is juicy, full flavoured, unctuous and sticky, with a garlicky, fruity kick that really complements the taste of the beef. It's so full of the flavours of Christmas that you really won't miss the turkey. It's particularly good served with red cabbage – a welcome relief for those who just don't see the point of sprouts (though the beef is good with sprouts too, or any other green veg for that matter). Major supermarkets sell ready-made spiced red cabbage dishes which can be bought ahead of time and often frozen. Or you can make your own and do the same. One less thing to worry about on the day. You can use either a boned and rolled joint of beef, or the full monty on-the-bone version. Each have much to recommend them – rolled is easier to handle (not to mention carve), on the bone is more awkward but tends to yield a fuller flavour and looks spectacularly traditional at the table – just what you want at Christmas!

As for the other dishes, well, two are no-cook options, leaving you more time to enjoy the festivities and the company of your guests – who wants to spend all of Christmas Day in the kitchen? If you're expecting vegetarian guests, there's an alternative dish for them too, which can be prepared before everyone arrives.

So here is an alternative menu for a great Christmas lunch or dinner. It's neither difficult nor scary, but it is delicious.

... what's the alternative?

By Sheila Hodgson, senior editor, Medical Romance™

WARM BLINIS WITH SMOKED SALMON, CRÈME FRAICHE AND CHIVES

I always think it's good to serve a simple pass-around type of starter to enjoy with a glass of something, cold, crisp and bubbly – enabling you and your guests to mingle, relax and get in the mood. Here is a no-cook, simple option.

INGREDIENTS

Ready-made cocktail blinis (available in packs from major supermarkets) Allow 3-4 per person.
200g (7oz) pot of crème fraîche
Bunch of chives or spring onions
200-400g (7-13 oz)pack of smoked salmon – allow 35g (1½ oz) per person
1 lemon

HOW TO MAKE

• Heat the oven to gas mark 6/200°C.
• Place blinis on a baking tray and place in oven for around 5 mins until heated through but still soft.
• Transfer to a warm plate.

• Top each blini with a tsp of crème fraîche and a roughly folded strip of smoked salmon (about 3 inches (7cm) long and an inch (2.5cm) wide).
• Spritz a few drops of lemon juice over each one.
• Finely chop the chives, or the trimmed green ends of spring onions, and sprinkle over the top.
• Serve immediately.

RIB OF BEEF WITH RED WINE, CRANBERRY AND GARLIC AND HERB-ROASTED WINTER VEGETABLES

INGREDIENTS
The meat
Either boned and rolled rib joint, or rib of beef on the bone. Allow 125–175g (4-6 oz) of raw rolled meat per person, or 250–375g (8-12 oz) if on the bone.
8-10 garlic cloves
150ml (¼pt) of red wine or port
60ml (4tbs) cranberry sauce or jelly
Salt and freshly ground black pepper
1tsp flour
½tsp of mustard powder

The vegetables
2 sprigs each of fresh thyme and rosemary

1kg (2 lbs potatoes)
(peeled, cut into large
chunks and boiled for 10
mins, allowed to cool then shaken to
roughen their edges. Make sure they
are cooled and well dried before
roasting)

½ a butternut squash – cut into cubes,
around same size as the potatoes

1 fennel bulb

1tbs vegetable oil, 2tbs of goose fat
(optional, if preferred substitute with
more vegetable oil)

The gravy

Up to 300ml (½ pint) of beef stock

5-10ml (1-2tsp) of plain flour
(depending upon amount of stock
used and how thick you like your
gravy!)

Salt and pepper to taste

HOW TO COOK

- First set oven at gas mark 7/220°C
- Weigh your meat
- Set meat in a roasting pan
- Cover the meat with the flour,
  mustard, salt and pepper
- Place in the middle of your oven
  and roast for 20 mins
- Scatter the cloves around the meat
- Reduce the heat to gas mark
  3/160°C and continue to cook for
  a further:

Well done 25-30 minutes per 500g (1lb)
Medium 20-25 minutes per 500g (1lb)
Rare 15-20 minutes per 500g(1lb)

- After 1 hour remove the garlic cloves from the oven. Allow to cool. Place the port or wine and cranberry sauce/jelly in a saucepan. Squeeze the garlic cloves and empty the pulp into the saucepan. Heat for 5 minutes until the cranberry sauce/ jelly has melted.
- 30 minutes before the end of the cooking time, baste the meat with a few tablespoonfuls of the cranberry mixture. Turn the oven up to Gas Mark 6/200°C Replace in the oven.
- Then heat the fat/oil in a roasting pan. Add the vegetables, seasoning and herbs and carefully turn together to coat the vegetables. Place on the top shelf of the oven for 40-45 minutes. Turn the vegetables over halfway through cooking time.
- 15 minutes after basting the meat with the cranberry mixture, repeat and return the meat to the oven for the final 15 minutes.
- At the end of the cooking time, remove the meat from the oven, and put on a hot plate, cover lightly with foil and leave in a warm place to rest until the vegetables are cooked and the gravy is made.
- Meanwhile make the gravy. Pour off most of the fat from the meat juices. Add the flour and stir over the heat until the flour has browned (make sure to incorporate the brown sediment, it has all the flavour). Add the stock and any remaining cranberry glaze mixture to the pan and stir until boiling. Season to taste
- Serve immediately.

STILTON AND MUSHROOM TART

A great vegetarian option, robust enough to stand up to the same accompaniments as the beef and can be made before your guests arrive.
(Serves 2-3)

INGREDIENTS
The pastry
125g (4oz) plain flour
pinch of salt
50g (2oz) butter
1 egg yolk
cold water

The filling
15g (1/2oz) butter
1/2 medium onion
1 clove garlic
125g (41/2oz) mushrooms
150ml (5fl oz) of single cream
1 egg and 1 egg yolk
125g (41/2oz) Stilton cheese
Chopped chives
Salt and freshly ground black pepper

HOW TO COOK
The pastry
- Sieve the flour and salt into a large mixing bowl.
- Add the butter.
- Rub together until resembling fine breadcrumbs
- Add the egg yolk and enough very cold water to bind together
- Roll out the pastry and line a 20cm/8inch flan ring
- Place in the fridge for 15 mins to relax
- Line the pastry case with foil and add a layer of dried beans
- Bake the pastry case blind in the

middle of the oven for 25-30 mins at gas mark 5/190°C, removing the foil and beans after 15 mins.

- Allow to cool. The pastry case can be made a day ahead and kept in an airtight box

The filling

- To make the filling, finely chop the onion and garlic and fry over a low heat in the butter for 3 minutes
- Slice the mushrooms and add to the onion and garlic, fry for 4–5 minutes on a higher heat until golden brown.
- Mix the cream and the whole egg and yolk together.
- Add the Stilton, chives and mushroom, onion and garlic mix.
- Pour the mixture into the flan case.
- Bake at gas mark 6/200°C for 30-40 minutes. Remove from the flan ring and bake for another five minutes.
- Best served just warm.

RASPBERRY, LEMON AND ALMOND TRIFLE

This recipe will serve 6-8 people – if you need to feed more then increase the quantities. Trifle is not an exact science. This is best made the day before and left in the fridge for its flavours to develop.

INGREDIENTS

500g (1lb) of frozen raspberries (thawed)
500g (1lb) carton of fresh custard
approx 12 soft Italian morbidi (soft macaroon biscuits)
4-6tbs sherry or brandy
2tbs lemon curd
raspberry jam
200g (7oz) mascarpone cheese
200g (7oz) half fat crème fraîche
50g (2oz) whole almonds

HOW TO MAKE
(You'll need a large deep bowl for this)
- Chop the almonds into slivers and grill or roast until golden brown (watch them like a hawk, they don't take long and burn quickly). Leave to cool
- Empty the raspberries into the bottom of the bowl
- Split the macaroons and sandwich back together with raspberry jam
- Top the raspberries with the macaroon sandwiches – in one layer
- Pour the sherry or brandy over the macaroons
- Pour the custard over the macaroons
- Mix the mascarpone and crème fraiche with the lemon curd until well incorporated
- With a palette knife, spread evenly over the custard
- Sprinkle with the toasted almonds
- Refrigerate until ready to eat

WORDSEARCH

B	B	L	P	W	S	S	E	N	R	E	H	T	E	G	O	T
N	Y	K	Y	G	L	O	W	V	H	R	R	K	N	T	R	Q
Q	S	R	M	C	C	A	F	F	E	C	T	I	O	N	Q	N
S	M	O	T	C	A	D	Y	R	A	R	O	M	A	N	C	E
U	E	Y	F	E	A	R	N	G	R	Q	R	G	T	R	L	H
O	N	N	M	T	O	N	E	A	T	N	L	E	S	N	I	L
R	G	O	M	L	M	P	D	S	H	V	N	E	D	N	Q	H
O	A	M	C	L	P	U	W	L	S	N	N	X	Y	N	U	V
M	P	R	T	H	K	Z	S	F	E	T	I	H	C	Q	E	B
A	M	A	H	Y	N	T	I	I	I	L	E	D	T	K	U	T
N	A	H	V	F	E	N	K	M	C	D	I	A	N	H	R	S
M	H	W	L	U	E	N	E	Z	I	B	E	G	C	A	Q	H
B	C	A	Q	W	G	N	H	S	M	S	L	N	H	P	H	A
X	M	U	I	N	T	P	E	H	E	K	F	D	M	T	X	R
E	O	N	X	T	M	R	V	V	N	V	Q	G	K	Q	G	I
B	E	R	T	H	I	C	O	C	K	T	A	I	L	S	N	N
C	N	M	W	F	N	L	R	Y	K	N	T	S	A	O	T	G

AFFECTION	FIRESIDE	POETRY
AMOROUS	FLAME	ROMANCE
BOUQUET	GLOW	SENTIMENT
CANDLELIGHT	HAND IN HAND	SHARING
CARESS	HARMONY	SOFT MUSIC
CHAMPAGNE	HEARTH	TENDER
COCKTAILS	LIQUEUR	TOAST
FINE WINE	LOVE SEAT	TOGETHERNESS

RINGING IN THE
New Year
WITH A
GLASS OF BUBBLY!

Tips for choosing champagne...or is it sparkling wine?

It's New Year's Eve and you and your friends plan to party with good food, music and of course, champagne! So a few days before the big night you visit the off licence... only to be overwhelmed by the dizzying assortment of champagnes and sparkling wines from all over the world. You could spend under £5 – or over £200 – a bottle. What's a person to do?

Strictly speaking, the only "true" champagne comes from the Marne Valley in the Champagne region of northeastern France. Other regions of France also make sparkling wine, but they aren't permitted to call it champagne.

But whether you call it champagne or sparkling wine, there's a bottle out there to suit your taste and budget! Expect to spend £25 to £40 for a good non-vintage champagne from one of the leading French producers such as Piper-Heidsieck, Moët & Chandon, Mumm, Taittinger and Perrier-Jouët.

These firms also offer vintage and premium champagnes at considerably higher prices. For example, a magnum of Dom Pérignon vintage 1993 (from Moët & Chandon) will cost over £200, and a bottle of their 1990 vintage rosé will set you back about £180.

But many of the leading French firms also own California wineries that produce excellent sparkling wines at more affordable prices:

Domaine Carneros (by Taittinger), Mumm Cuvée Napa Brut Prestige and Piper Sonoma Select Cuvée are highly rated bottles that can be found for £10 or less. Similarly, supermarkets are cornering the market in sparkling wine at great prices.

The problem with many inexpensive sparkling wines is that they are too sweet. The key to buying a less expensive sparkling wine is to take the advice of a serious wine merchant... and experiment. Perfectly delicious sparkling wines can be had for £10 or less. Try an Italian Prosecco or a Spanish Cava – you'll be glad you did!

"Remember, gentlemen, it's not just France we're fighting for, it's champagne."
Winston Churchill, 1918

Selecting a sparkling wine is much easier when you understand the information printed on the label. Here are a few basics:

Appellation d'Origine Contrôlée (AOC)

Indicates where a French wine was made and certifies that it was made according to regional regulations.

Vintage

The harvest year of the grapes. Most champagnes are made from a blend of grapes from several different years and so are non-vintage.

Méthode champenoise or fermented in this bottle

Indicates that the champagne was made in the traditional, labour-intensive manner, with the second fermentation taking place in the bottle in which the wine will be sold.

Charmat method

Indicates that the sparkling wine was made by a less expensive method, with the second fermentation taking place in a closed vat.

Level of sweetness

Indicated on the label. "Brut" means dry; "extra brut" or "ultra brut" means drier yet. "Extra dry" is sweeter than "brut," and "sec," "demi-sec," and "doux" are sweeter yet.

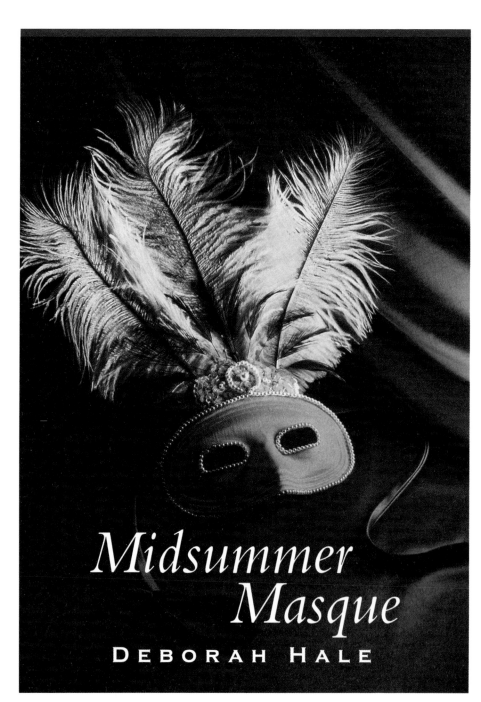

Midsummer
Masque

DEBORAH HALE

Northamptonshire, England, 1818

He had waited so long for her.

Lord Auberon Westborne gazed across his travelling carriage at Miss Sylvie Somerville, presently in animated conversation with her lady's maid. When she laughed, tendrils of dark hair that peeped from beneath her bonnet danced.

Had he waited too long? Lord Westborne feared so.

Ever since he could remember, an eventual match between the two of them had been an unspoken certainty on the part of their families. And ever since she had made an effort to ease the social torture of a party for him six years ago, his heart had been hers. She'd been so young then. A mere girl of seventeen, while he had been in his twenties and years older still in experience and responsibility.

Knowing she thought of him only as a dear, old friend or courtesy elder brother, he had scrupulously avoided revealing the intensity of his feelings, for fear of frightening her away. She would be his one day and he had been content to wait, anticipating.

Sylvie looked up suddenly and caught him watching her. Two bewitching dimples blossomed on either side of her equally bewitching lips. "My dear West, you look positively grim! I hope you have not got a toothache, poor fellow. I would hate to have this lovely visit with your cousin spoiled for you."

She did not blush when she spoke, which troubled Lord Westborne. A young lady should blush if she discovered a man staring at her with the transparent longing he feared his face must betray. At least, she should if she had the slightest romantic interest in the fellow.

"My teeth are quite sound, thank you." He wasn't in his dotage yet. Though perhaps he might as well be as far as she was concerned.

He admitted a half-truth to explain his solemn countenance. "I was only thinking about this sudden engagement of Daventry's and wondering what it all means."

They were on their way to a house party at Helmhurst, the country estate of Lord Westborne's cousin, Lucius Daventry, to celebrate the baron's betrothal. The culmination of the gathering was to be a splendid masquerade ball. West had accepted the invitation eagerly, hoping the romantic atmosphere might make Sylvie more receptive to the notion of him as a lover and a husband.

When she had returned to England recently after a year abroad, West had fallen in love all over again, for she had matured into the clever, vivacious, beautiful woman he'd always known she would. Exultant that his time had come at last, he'd been crushed to discover she had no wish to encourage his romantic attentions. Nor ever to wed him.

"Why, it means Lord Daventry has met a special lady and fallen in love with her, I hope." Sylvie's gaze strayed out the carriage window to drink in the lush hedgerows of England's heartland. The wistful look on her delicate features made West ache to hold her. "I am so happy for him, poor man, after what happened to him during the war, and how cruel everyone has been since."

She glanced back at West again, an unexpected glint of steel in her dreamy blue eyes. "No one who called him Lord Lucifer in my hearing was ever fool enough to do it a second time!"

West laughed, in spite of his burdened heart. That was one of the things he'd always loved about Sylvie — her spirit, her loyalty and her kind heart. Though it was on account of those latter admirable qualities that he dared not show her the true depth of his feelings. If she knew of his dogged devotion, she would do anything to keep from hurting him. Even if that meant wedding him against her inclination. He cared for her happiness far too much to let that happen.

But perhaps the exposure to his cousin's happy betrothal would make her reconsider, and give him the smile or word of encouragement he had craved for so long.

Lord Westborne had the kindest eyes, and the saddest, too. Sylvie had always thought so. Even as a young girl she had

sought to draw him out, to make him laugh and enjoy himself a little. Though otherwise the very best of men, he had always been too shy and too solemn.

"I wonder how Lord Daventry came to meet this Miss Lacewood?" she mused. "I heard he never goes anywhere, and then only in the dead of night."

She remembered Lucius Daventry as he had been before Waterloo. "The Handsomest Beau in Britain" everyone had called him then. Sylvie had heartily agreed, though she'd always thought Lord Westborne's face had more character. She hoped her own face would not betray any aversion when she met the baron again and saw the black mask with which he concealed his war wounds.

The carriage turned off the main road just then onto a long lane that led to a magnificent old house.

Lord Westborne shrugged. "From what I can gather, the young lady is a neighbour of theirs. I believe she took a kind interest in the earl while Lucius was off to war. I would not put it past the old fellow to have had a hand in matchmaking for the two of them."

"His fiancée is someone Lord Daventry has known all his life, you mean?" The information surprised Sylvie. "Then perhaps it is not a love match after all."

No one could fall in love with a person they had known all their lives. She was certain of that. For some time now, she had been waiting and expecting to fall in love — the kind of love she had heard extolled in poem and play, song and story. She'd hoped that during her year abroad she might meet someone special to whom she could surrender her heart. There had been men who'd made that organ flutter for an hour or two, but it had not taken them long to fall short of her ideal. Though West might think her a frivolous creature, she wanted more in a husband than good looks and a flattering tongue.

She knew her family planned for her to marry Lord Westborne, but that was out of the question. Wealthy, well bred, handsome and kind, he had been a fixture in her life for as long as she could recall. How could one fall in love with a fixture?

"I only hope Daventry's fiancée is not after his fortune," West muttered.

He was so devoted to his family, what little he had. That was one of the things Sylvie liked best about him. Though she feared he might let his strong sense of duty spoil his own chance to fall in love. He had never shown the least interest in her as a woman, yet he was vastly attentive in a brotherly fashion. If she permitted it, she feared he would drift into marriage with her to fulfill a family obligation. Not an unpleasant one, perhaps, but not the kind

of romantic rapture she wished for him...and for herself.

Perhaps if his cousin's engagement were a love match, West would see that he must not allow himself to settle for less. If, on the other hand, Lord Daventry and Miss Lacewood had contracted an alliance on some other basis, it might serve as a warning for what West should avoid.

For her part, Sylvie could not help hoping true love might find her at Lord Daventry's midsummer masque!

CHAPTER 2

A foolish sense of satisfaction and hope budded inside Lord Auberon Westborne as he helped Sylvie Somerville out of his carriage. Bringing her to Helmhurst to help celebrate his cousin's engagement made him feel as if she belonged to him, however briefly.

The Earl of Welland stood near the magnificent pillared entrance to the house, greeting his guests. The old fellow looked as frail as ever, but happier than West had seen him since his grandson had returned disfigured after the Battle of Waterloo. Beside the earl stood a lovely young woman with golden hair and a shy smile.

"Westborne, my dear boy!" The earl glanced from West to Sylvie with the twinkling eyes of an unrepentant matchmaker. "I am delighted you've brought such a lovely companion with you to grace our celebrations. I want this gloomy old place steeped to the eaves in the laughter and romance of young folk for a few days. It will be the perfect tonic for me."

West dearly hoped he would be able to oblige the old fellow. He bowed to the earl and to the young lady he assumed must be his cousin's fiancée. "Thank you for the invitation, sir. May I present a dear friend of the family, Miss Sylvie Somerville?"

"What — not Bram Somerville's little girl? Why it seems just yesterday we were toasting your christening. Welcome, my dear!" The earl turned to the young woman beside him. "This is a dear friend of my family, and soon to be a member of it, Miss Angela Lacewood."

The gentlemen bowed over the ladies' hands. West and Sylvie both congratulated Miss Lacewood on her engagement to Lord Daventry and everyone praised the fine weather.

"Is Lucius around, by any chance?" asked West. "I'd like to congratulate him on his good fortune and good sense in securing such a lovely bride."

"You'll see him at dinner," said the earl with no further explanation. "Until then, why don't you both settle in and make yourselves at home. I hope you brought masks and costumes for the ball."

They assured him that, indeed, they had. West could scarcely wait for a glimpse of Sylvie as Helen of Troy. He'd have launched a thousand ships for her, if he'd thought it would do him any good.

"So what do you think of Miss Lacewood?" Sylvie whispered once they were out of earshot. "Is she in love with your cousin, do you suppose?"

"That is hardly the sort of thing one can tell from a brief meeting." Or even a long acquaintance. Otherwise Sylvie would have realised ages ago how much he cared for her. Perhaps she didn't want to see it.

"I suppose not." Sylvie did not appear convinced. "She is very lovely, though. Whatever may have induced her to accept Lord Daventry, I do not believe it was his fortune."

"My mind is at rest on that score as well," West agreed. "What shall we do to amuse ourselves until dinner? Would you care to take a stroll through the gardens? Helmhurst has very fine ones."

"We've been cooped up in your carriage together all the way from home." An anxious look tightened Sylvie's smile. Did she think a walk in the gardens might give him unwanted encouragement? "Why not mingle with some of the other guests? The earl told me they're set up for pall-mall and tennis."

"Pall-mall it is." West tried not to let his disappointment show. After all, any time spent in Sylvie's company was a rare boon, even if he had to share her attention.

It had been a most enjoyable afternoon, Sylvie decided as she dressed for dinner. She and West had won their match against Viscount Allingham and his sister. West had been vastly comical, larking about with his mallet and pretending to get the wickets mixed up. It was good to see the dear fellow relaxing and enjoying himself.

Once or twice, her gaze had met Viscount Allingham's as they'd chuckled over Lord Westborne's antics, and she had felt a blush rise to her cheeks. The viscount was very handsome and charming. His sister might do quite well for West...except that she had a rather tart tongue. Sylvie did not want to see her dear friend saddled with a scold for a wife.

She was delighted to find herself seated between West and the viscount at dinner. It was a rather strange meal, though.

"Why so few candles?" she whispered to West as the soup was being served.

"It's Lucius." West nodded towards the foot of the table where his cousin sat. "The earl tells me his injured eye is painfully sensitive to bright light."

"How awful for him." Hard as she tried, Sylvie could not keep her sympathy untainted by a tiny qualm of fear. Lord Daventry's black mask did give him a rather diabolical appearance. "I wonder how poor Miss Lacewood will manage, wed to a man who must live his life in darkness?"

She should have kept her voice down. A striking redhead sitting on West's right, leaned towards them and purred with gleeful malice, "Don't you think that might be one of the attractions of the match for her? Imagine a wealthy husband one hardly ever needs to keep company with!"

West made some sort of vague comment about doubting Lord Daventry's fiancée would agree, while Sylvie struggled to rein in her indignation.

If she hadn't thought it would make a dreadful scene, she'd have been tempted to dump the contents of her soup bowl over the little minx!

Sylvie knew the creature, if only by reputation. Lady Esmé Talbot had jilted two men already, and only her father's wealth and title had kept her from being shunned by the ton. Fearing Lady Esmé might have designs on West, Sylvie took care to keep him so engaged in conversation with her that he scarcely had a moment to glance at his right-hand neighbour.

If that meant she had no time to chat with Viscount Allingham, it couldn't be helped. A lady must be willing to make some sacrifices for the man she…liked a great deal. Sylvie felt quite rewarded when, near the end of the meal, the viscount stole an opportunity to whisper an intriguing invitation.

By the end of dinner, West felt as if he had drunk too much of the earl's fine wine. Sylvie's sudden exclusive interest set him giddy with hope. Why, she'd hardly even glanced at that coxcomb Allingham, who'd been taking far too much interest in her to suit West.

Perhaps his foolishness during their game that afternoon had made her see he wasn't as stuffy and backward as she might have thought. Or perhaps there was a little magic in the air. West didn't care what was behind it, as long as it worked.

When the gentlemen retired to the earl's library, West excused himself as soon as he could. He tipped the earl's ancient valet a large sum for information about Miss Somerville's whereabouts, then raced to the gardens in search of her.

Just as he was rounding one of the hedges, he heard her cry, "So you did come, after all!"

West opened his mouth to reply. Before he could speak, another man's voice answered the very words he'd meant to say. "My apologies, dear lady. I came as soon as I could."

"You're here now," said Sylvie. "That's what matters."

As West watched from behind the hedge, his hope shattered and ground into the dust, the woman he loved took Allingham's arm and they began a slow stroll around the garden.

CHAPTER 3

He should not listen, Lord Westborne told himself as he stood behind a laurel hedge while his beloved Sylvie flirted with Viscount Allingham on the other side. Such conduct was beneath a gentleman. Nor did he want to hear what they might say. His heart pained him quite enough already.

But when he tried to move, his legs would not cooperate.

"What kept you?" Sylvie asked Allingham in a tone of sweet mock-petulance. "I was beginning to think you might not come after all."

"If you believe I'd prefer standing around a stuffy library drinking port to strolling with you under the stars, you are not nearly as clever a woman as I took you for, Miss Somerville."

She gave a silvery little laugh. The kind West had congratulated himself on prompting that afternoon. Was that rascal, Allingham, kissing her hand or taking some other minor liberty? Where Sylvie was concerned, there were no minor liberties.

"You flatter me, sir," she said. "I am not nearly as accomplished as your sister."

Now Allingham laughed. "There's a difference between cleverness and being a know-it-all little bluestocking. It was most unkind of you not to rescue me from one of Jane's tiresome lectures during dinner. You were paying me so little heed, I was afraid I'd done something to offend you."

"Never!" insisted Sylvie. "I had to keep Lord Westborne talking so Lady Esmé wouldn't get her claws into him. I want the dear fellow to find a nice wife, not take up with some dreadful little minx who'll break his heart."

West clenched his teeth to keep from crying out. There was only one wife he wanted. A hundred Lady Esmés could not have tempted him. Nor hurt him more cruelly, with so little intention.

Gradually, Sylvie and the viscount sauntered almost out of earshot. West could hear only the muted cadence of their conversation, frequently punctuated by Sylvie's laughter. He tried to steal away so he would not be discovered and humiliated. His legs continued to defy his will. He was still rooted to the same spot when Sylvie and Allingham came closer again.

"In that case, may I have the honour of a dance at the ball?" the viscount asked.

"More than one if you wish," replied Sylvie. "So you have no trouble finding me, I shall be costumed as Helen of Troy."

"How very apt." The caressing tone of Allingham's voice made West yearn to vault over the hedge and throttle him. "Not that you need to have told me. I would have picked you out of the throng no matter what costume or mask you wore."

"I dare not make such a boast, sir," said Sylvie. "So you had better tell me what you will be wearing. Otherwise, I might accept an invitation from the wrong gentleman."

"You must accept no one but Robin Hood, fair Helen. But be warned, he is a scoundrel who may try to steal a kiss."

"Be warned, Lord Allingham." Sylvie's voice had a teasing, almost seductive note that West would have given anything to hear addressed to him. "He may not need to steal it."

Once again, they wandered away. Farther this time, for West could no longer hear them at all. His rebellious legs finally decided to operate again. He managed to stagger into the house and up to his room, where he hurled himself face down on the bed.

How he wished he were a child again so he could summon the tears that might have eased his parched heart.

Sylvie was too keyed-up to sleep. After

returning from her starlight stroll in the garden with Viscount Allingham, she had gone straight to bed. After what seemed like hours of tossing and turning, she had concluded it was useless to keep lying there.

This strange unease that kept her awake — could it be love? She asked herself that question as she rose, lit a candle, then donned her dressing gown. If it was, she wondered what all the fuss in books and ballads was about.

Perhaps she hadn't given it a proper chance to flourish, though. All the while she'd been walking with the viscount, part of her mind had been wondering if West was with the other gentlemen in the library or whether he might be strolling elsewhere on the grounds with a young lady on his arm. She would have heartily approved, provided it was not Lady Esmé...or Jane Allingham...or that toplofty Miss Whiteside...or...

Might there be a scullery maid still awake in the kitchen who could warm her a cup of milk? Sylvie hated to think of disturbing anyone. Perhaps she could creep down to the earl's library and borrow a book to read. Something nice and tiresome that would put her to sleep after a few pages.

Easing the guest room door open, she padded down the corridor, her bare feet making scarcely a sound on the thick carpet. As she rounded the corner that led to the west wing of the house, she collided with someone hurrying in the opposite direction.

Large, powerful hands closed around her arms to keep her from falling. Fumbling her candle, she barely managed to stifle a scream.

"West?" she asked in a loud whisper, holding the candle higher. "Is that you? What are you doing up at this hour?"

The moment the words left her lips, she wished she could recall them. Was it not obvious what the man must be doing — prowling around at a country-house party in the middle of the night?

He looked it, too. His warm brown hair was dishevelled, his neck linen was gone and his loose white shirt hung open, exposing a deep wedge of bare chest. Had Lord Westborne been dallying with one of the ladies? The notion took Sylvie's breath away.

"I might ask you the same question." West's voice had a harsh huskiness she'd never heard before. If she hadn't known him so long and so well, it might have alarmed her. "Where are you going at this hour?"

"To get a book from the library, if you must know." Considering what he might be up to, he had no business quizzing her in that gruff tone. "I'm having a devil of a time getting to sleep." Where did he think she was bound?

Her indignation evaporated when she

looked into his eyes. The green in them seemed to blaze with verdant fury, while the brown ached with anguish too deep for words.

"Is something wrong?" She tried to reach out to him, only to realise he was still holding tight to her arms.

The candle flame between them danced wildly. If they weren't careful, one of them might get badly burned.

"You can let go of me now," she whispered, though her knees felt weak all of a sudden. Perhaps it was the fright from bumping into him in the dark.

He glanced down with a puzzled look, as if his hands were acting on their own, contrary to his will. "F-forgive me. I didn't mean to —"

What could have happened to distress him so? "Can I help, West? Whatever is the matter, I hope you know you can always confide in me."

He threw his head back, shaking with silent, frenzied laughter. The next thing Sylvie knew, he pushed past her and fled down the corridor. But not before the light of her candle glinted off a hint of mist in his haunted eyes.

CHAPTER 4

What had he done? Lord Westborne blundered down the darkened corridor with Sylvie's parting words echoing in his ears. "Whatever is the matter, I hope you know you can always confide in me."

Heaven help him, she was the last person in whom he could ever confide. For she was both his problem and the impossible solution to it.

How could he stay for the ball to celebrate his cousin's engagement when it was certain to mean watching Viscount Allingham make a conquest of the woman West loved? He'd sooner be hanged.

An air of brooding silence hung over the sleeping house. West had to get outside where he could breathe and where the night air might cool his fever of self-reproach.

What must Sylvie think of him after the way he'd acted? Had he angered her? Frightened her? Repelled her with his raw emotions the way she might have cowered from the sight of a gaping, gushing wound? Whatever her reaction, he had probably driven her straight into his rival's arms.

He was wandering on the south lawn, drowning in regrets, when a familiar masculine voice reached out of the darkness. "Who's there?"

"Lucius?" West stopped. "Is that you?"

"Oh, West." His cousin sounded relieved.

"I've hardly had a chance for a word with you. It was good of you to come. I hope you and Miss Somerville are enjoying yourselves."

West tried to mouth a polite falsehood, but he could not.

"Ah," said Lucius in a knowing tone. "Anything I can do?"

If he didn't tell someone, he might explode, as he had very nearly done with Sylvie. "Care to give a fellow a little advice in matters of the heart?"

Lucius gave a soft, raspy chuckle. West could imagine his cousin's dark brow raised. "I am hardly an expert on the subject."

"You must know something, though, securing such a lovely fiancée." In spite of his marred looks and his suspect reputation.

"What's the trouble then?" asked Lucius. "I won't pretend I have any wisdom to offer. Now and then it just does a man good to get it all out. Like a thorough purging."

Something about the confessional atmosphere of the night's warm darkness coaxed West to speak. "It's Miss Somerville, as I expect you've guessed."

"She appeared very attentive to you at dinner."

"Only to keep me from talking to the Talbot chit."

"Still, isn't that encouraging?"

West shook his head, then remembered Lucius couldn't see him. "You don't understand."

He only meant to offer a few words of explanation, but everything came spewing out. West could no more have stopped it than he could have paused in the middle of being violently ill. His cousin had been right about one thing, though. Once it was no longer all inside, eating away at him, he felt a good deal better.

After a moment's thoughtful silence, Lucius asked, "Have you told any of this to Miss Somerville?"

"Have you not heeded a word I've said?" West cried. "Of course I haven't told her. Have you told Miss Lacewood how you feel about her?"

"We aren't talking about me, though I understand what you mean. I don't pretend it will be easy. Sometimes the more a man cares for a woman, the harder it is for him to woo her."

"I thought you had no wisdom to impart, Lucius."

"Promise me something?"

"What?"

"If an opportunity arises for you to woo Miss Somerville, you'll seize it."

Precious little fear of that! "I will. Thank you, Lucius. I hope you and Miss

Lacewood will be very happy together."

Lucius did not answer. But on the mild night air, West thought he heard a faint sigh. Was there more to his cousin's betrothal than met the eye? West wondered. Or perhaps...less?

Sylvie sighed. Then she yawned. She would need a good nap this afternoon or she'd never be able to stay awake for the ball. Poor West looked like he could use a rest, too. She told him as much at breakfast.

He treated her to a withering look over the brim of his coffee cup. "If you mean I look a wreck, go ahead and say it."

Sylvie swept a glance around at the few other guests who had gathered in Helmhurst's smaller dining room. "I didn't mean any such thing and you know it."

She did not want to quarrel with him, but fatigue and bewilderment had frayed her temper. Last night she had glimpsed a side of Auberon Westborne she'd never guessed. It had stirred something in her that she was reluctant to examine too closely. Something that her pleasant flirtation with Viscount Allingham had not roused in the least.

"Is everything all right?" She kept her voice low to avoid drawing too much attention. "I could see you weren't yourself last night."

"I am always myself, Sylvie." His tone stung her. "Though perhaps not always

the man you like to think I am."

"Please." She pressed her fingers to her temple. "It's too early in the morning for talking in riddles."

West rose abruptly. "Then perhaps you should go find Allingham. His manner of talk seems to suit you better than mine. And you needn't feel you have to hover around to protect me from some predatory vixen. I'm perfectly able to take care of myself."

He stalked off, leaving the other guests staring, and Sylvie as shocked as if he'd hurled the tea urn at her.

What had come over West? Whatever did he mean about not being the man she thought he was? As her weary mind absorbed his words about Viscount Allingham and predatory vixens, she grew more and more distressed. West must have overheard her talking with the viscount last evening.

Was it possible Lord Westborne had deeper feelings for her than she'd ever realised?

And if she had been mistaken about that, was it possible she'd been mistaken in her own feelings as well?

"This isn't the mask and costume I brought!" West stared at the garments laid out on his bed.

He had planned to go as King Arthur.

This looked like...

West's valet shook his head, as if to say it was none of his doing. "The earl's man brought it around, sir. Said it was compliments of Lord Daventry."

Suddenly it all made sense. "I suppose he took my gear away with him?"

"Should I not have given it to him, sir? He said it was orders from the baron. I thought you must know."

"Never mind, Charters. I'll make do." Under his breath West muttered, "Damn you, Lucius!"

Seize his chance to woo Sylvie, indeed. There lay his chance, right down to the quiver full of arrows, which he might use like Cupid, to pierce Miss Somerville's indifferent heart. Did he dare try?

Apart from encasing his troublesome emotions in a stout shell of reason and responsibility, he had little experience with deception and even less taste for it. Was any woman worth stooping to such depths for?

He had firmly decided not — made up his mind he wouldn't attend the ball. Who would miss him, after all? Then, from out in the corridor, he heard Sylvie's laughter chime. The sound left him dizzy and breathless.

Did he not owe it to himself, and perhaps to her, to try? If she discovered his deception, she might hate him, but West preferred that to the prospect of having

her wed him out of pity.

"Well, what are we waiting for, Charters? I have a masquerade to attend."

And a fair damsel to win.

CHAPTER 5

If ever there had been a night meant for lovers, this one was!

Dressed as Helen of Troy in a flowing Greek chiton, Sylvie Somerville watched with a smile on her lips and a gentle mist in her eyes when Lord Daventry and his fiancée made their entrance at the masquerade ball celebrating their engagement.

When Sylvie and Lord Westborne had arrived the previous day, she'd wondered if this match between the scarred war veteran and his beautiful neighbour could possibly be based on love. Watching the way Miss Lacewood clung to Lord Daventry's arm, and his visible pride in her, all Sylvie's doubts had been banished.

Apparently it was possible for two people who had known each other a long time to fall in love. Until yesterday, Sylvie had believed it quite out of the question. Now she gazed around the darkening south lawn, where the ball was being held, and savoured the atmosphere of romantic possibility.

Music wafted on the warm evening air

from a small but skilful orchestra. Guests in colourful costumes made intricate shifting patterns on the tiled terrace that served as a dance floor. Tiny tin lanterns cast twinkling light from the branches of the trees that surrounded the lawn, mirroring the stars that were beginning to appear in the darkening sky above.

A masculine voice with a mellow, musical cadence wrapped around her from behind, shimmering with admiration. "Helen, 'fairer than the evening air clad in the beauty of a thousand stars!'"

A delicious blush suffused her cheeks and she spun about to face...Robin Hood? For an instant, she had thought the voice belonged to someone other than Viscount Allingham. But, of course, it couldn't.

Fortunately her mask helped obscure any flicker of disappointment that might have crossed her face. What was there to be disappointed about, after all? She had agreed to meet the viscount here tonight and spend the evening with him.

"Why, Robin Hood, you are curiously eloquent for an outlaw." Hard as she tried to recapture the bubbly banter of the previous evening, it eluded her. "I hope you do not mean to steal from me." She twirled around, making the soft folds of bleached muslin billow around her. "As you can see, I have little worth taking."

"Quite the contrary, my dear." He held out his arm to her. "You have riches beyond price. To gaze on your beauty, to hear your laughter, to bask in your smile — all are treasures of the highest value."

His voice rang with a sweet note of sincerity that Sylvie found difficult to resist.

She tucked her hand into the crook of his elbow. "But you need not filch any of those, Sir Robin. They are yours to have when you will."

"Perhaps, but there are other prizes of even rarer value." He nodded towards the terrace and began to walk in that direction. "A dance, for instance?"

"You would steal a dance?"

He glanced towards her with a smile of such tender reverence that it set her heart aflutter. "Ah, there's the rub. Like so many of life's most precious riches, it would lose all its worth unless given freely."

There was something different in his manner that touched her. Could she be feeling the stirrings of true love, at last?

She clutched his arm a little tighter. "If you set such great store by it, then I would be honoured to grant what you ask."

They took their places among the other dancers, waiting for the orchestra to strike up the next tune. "Take care, my dear. There are treasures you possess that you must not surrender simply because someone else desires them."

The air filled with music, and a sprightly country dance swept them up before

Sylvie could ask what he meant. But each time his hand closed over hers, each time their bodies brushed in the most innocent contact, each time she glanced up to find his gaze caressing her, a quiver of delicious elation beyond anything poets had tried to capture with words ran through her.

After several dances, Sylvie and her partner revived themselves with champagne and assorted delicacies from the buffet. Then they danced again. By turns flirtatious, gallant and tender, Robin Hood seemed intent upon stealing her heart.

Only when she recalled the haunted look in Lord Westborne's eyes did Sylvie feel a pang of remorse. But wait? Did she glimpse something sweetly familiar, yet deliciously novel, in the masked eyes of her dancing partner?

Could it be there was more to Robin Hood — and Lord Westborne — than met the eye?

Had someone sprinkled stardust over him and Sylvie and this whole enchanted night? For the first time since his earliest childhood, Lord Westborne felt ready to believe in magic.

His mask and costume gave him a safe bastion from behind which to mount his romantic conquest. A counterfeit persona liberated him to speak the words he had hoarded in his heart for so long. Sylvie's ardent responses emboldened him to risk everything on this desperate gamble to win her.

The way she held his arm, the way she smiled, the subtle caress in her voice when she spoke to him, all convinced West she could love him. All she'd needed was a chance to see him with fresh eyes.

"Another dance?" he nodded towards the terrace.

Sylvie considered for a moment, then shook her head. "I have enjoyed dancing with you very much and I hope we may share many more in the future. But I have grown a trifle weary for tonight."

She wasn't going to leave already? West wanted this night with her to last at least until dawn. "More champagne, then?"

"I mustn't. I have had almost too much as it is."

She did want to leave. West's heart sank, though he chided himself for being greedy of her company. This night had given him more than he'd dared hope for when he'd accepted Lord Daventry's invitation.

Still he could not resist trying for more. "Almost too much may be just enough."

"In that case, I have had just enough and should not indulge any further."

"As you wish, then." He tried to stifle a sigh but did not fully succeed. "Good night. Our time together has meant more to me than you will ever know."

He stooped to kiss her hand.

While his lips pressed to her fingers, unable to part from them, she slowly raised her hand. "Good night? I have no wish to end our pleasant interlude so soon, sir."

"You haven't?"

"Indeed, not." She caught her lower lip between her teeth for a moment. "I was hoping we might take a little stroll together under the stars. If you are willing?"

If? A whole bottle of champagne could not have set him so delightfully befuddled as her unexpected invitation. "I would be honoured."

West lost all track of time as they walked arm in arm in the starlight, talking about everything and nothing. He felt as if he knew Sylvie better after this one evening than after all the years of their acquaintance. She was everything he had hoped and more. Every second in her company, he fell a little further under her spell.

At last they found themselves wrapped in the magical perfume of a slumbering rose garden. An expectant hush fell over them and Lord Westborne knew the moment was right. Taking Sylvie in his arms, he kissed her in the way he'd waited so long to do. His kiss claimed her as his own, even as it offered himself to be her willing subject for the rest of his life.

Yet even in this sweet fulfilment of his dream, a tiny doubt bedevilled him. Would Sylvie be responding with such innocent passion to his kiss if she knew his true identity?

CHAPTER 6

Sylvie Somerville was not some green girl. She had been kissed before, on several occasions. How could a lady hope to discover true love if she kept every gentleman at arm's length? Besides, she had a lively curiosity about the passionate side of relationships between men and women. Some of the kisses she'd received had not been very pleasant. Others had been quite pleasant indeed.

The kiss she experienced now, in a starlit rose garden on an enchanted midsummer night, was so different from all the others it might have been another act altogether. Sylvie felt instinctively that this was her first kiss of true love, and she vowed it would not be her last!

The gentleman of her dreams held her in an embrace as tender and yearning as it was strong and protective. At first, his lips brushed against hers with the gentle delicacy of a butterfly's wing or the first warm breeze of spring. More than all the words in the world, his kiss assured her she was a rare and wondrous lady. Like the chivalrous knights of old, he would give her his whole heart in homage, asking nothing in return but permission to cherish her.

Sylvie was not some damsel in a tower, however, content to be admired from afar. She repented if she had ever let him think so. Pressing her lips to his with greater urgency, at the same time she let them melt against his with a subtle quiver that begged for more. He did not hesitate to oblige her, but swept her up in a masterful embrace, beguiling her to part her lips so he could push their kiss to breathtaking depths. Sylvie yielded to him with a sigh of exultant surrender.

Their kiss held all the comfort and contentment of homecoming while promising a lifetime of new discoveries and thrilling adventures to delight her.

She had been right to wait for this — to wait for him. If only she had not been wrong about so much else!

"Please don't stop!" she gasped when he drew back a little. She wanted nothing to wake either of them from this midsummer night's dream into which they'd strayed.

"Wed me, then!" He rained kisses on her ear and neck as he spoke. "And I will never stop."

The featherlight graze of his lips against her skin tickled in the most delightful way. How might it feel on other parts of her body?

"Wed?" A froth of laughter bubbled out of her. "Is this not rather sudden?"

"Not half soon enough." He continued to ply kisses down her neck and over her bare shoulder. "I have waited for you too long."

The rasp of unrequited desire in his voice roused Sylvie, even while she reproached herself. Cradling his face in her hands, she crooned her reply. "I have waited all my life for you."

"Let's not tarry a moment longer, then." His hand ran through the cascade of curls that tumbled from her headdress.

"What?" she gasped. "Run away to Gretna at this hour?" Not that she would hesitate if it were the only means of making him hers.

The passionate haste of an elopement appealed to her romantic spirit. But there was a furtive and selfish side to it as well. She wanted their family and friends to share in their joy. She wanted the whole world to see her pride in becoming his wife.

The warm weight of Sylvie in his arms made Lord Westborne quite delirious.

He shook his head in answer to her question about eloping. "Even that would not be soon enough for me."

"Then how...?" She subsided in a gurgle of delight as he returned to kissing her shoulders.

"A ceremony is only...the witnessing." He kept his lips in contact with her rose-petal skin, so that every word became a kiss. "What truly makes a man and woman husband and wife is the vows they make to one another. Will you make those vows with me, here? Every star in the heavens can bear witness."

"Wed in a rose garden at midnight?" She lingered over the words. "How vastly romantic!"

She was a creature of romance. No wonder she had given him no encouragement over the years. He had given her none — not a look or a word or a touch to convey the slightest hint of his true feelings for her.

Nor had he been truthful with himself about the reason for his reticence. At first he'd blamed his hesitation on her youth, blinding himself to her blossoming womanhood. Then he'd pretended to protect her from her own tender heart, when in truth it was his heart that needed protection. He had been prepared to wait and hope and pine for Sylvie — expecting her to give him some encouragement, rather than risk revealing his love in case she might tell him she could never return it.

If his cousin Lucius had not pushed him into it, would West be here with her now, a word away from gaining his heart's desire?

"Well?" he prompted her. "Will you?"

"How could I refuse?"

"Very easily, I'm afraid. But I hope you won't." More than he had hoped for anything in his life.

"Never fear." She traced his lips with the tip of her forefinger. Then she spoke the three most beautiful words West had ever heard. "I am yours."

He took her hands in his. "I promise, by all the stars in the heavens and by all the love in my heart, I will honour and cherish you as my wife forever."

"That's lovely! Much nicer than the words they make you say in church." The warmth of her breath caressed his face. "I promise, by all the stars in the heavens and by all the love in my heart, I will honour and cherish you as my husband forever."

She was his at long last! A great warm wave of relief threatened to knock West off his feet. "You have made me the happiest person in the world!"

"The happiest man, perhaps," Sylvie corrected him with an impish chuckle.

"Aye." West swept her into his arms again. "The very happiest man!"

He kissed her again with all the unappeased hunger that had once gnawed at his heart. The assurance that she returned his feelings made him bolder. His hands ranged over her, acquainting him with every delectable curve of her body through the fine muslin of her gown.

The ragged gust of her breath, the way she draped herself against him, her sighs of pleasure, convinced him of her matching desire.

She trembled in his arms.

"Are you cold, my love?" He gathered her closer to him...if that were possible. "Can I fetch you a wrap? Or do you wish to go inside?"

Sylvie shook her head. "I am not cold. I am on fire. The only wrap I want is your arms. I do want to go inside, though."

West struggled to contain his disappointment.

"To my bed," whispered Sylvie. "But only if you promise to join me."

"Join you?" West nearly dropped her. "In bed?"

"Why not?" Delicious, teasing laughter rippled through her. "We just wed, didn't we?"

West's mouth went dry. His body, already roused to an extremity he could barely stand, responded to her invitation. "Yes, but —"

"I want my wedding night, husband." She tugged him towards the house. "And I cannot wait."

All his life, Lord Westborne had been a careful, guarded, responsible fellow. Scores of prudent reasons to resist her tempting invitation clamoured in his mind. But they were no match for the love that swelled in his heart, or the ache of desire that racked his body.

"Neither can I!"

CHAPTER 7

Would she be doing this if she had a little less champagne inside her? The notion flitted through Sylvie Somerville's mind while she and her "bridegroom" stole into the darkened house. Meanwhile, the masked ball to celebrate Lord Daventry's engagement continued out on the south lawn.

A few moments earlier the lovers had made private vows of marriage in the rose garden, under the stars. While all very romantic, those vows would not protect Sylvie from scandal if her new husband declined to repeat them later in front of human witnesses.

The moment she latched her bedroom door behind them and he folded her in his embrace, all her doubts fled. He was not the one who'd suggested this tryst. It was she who had been unwilling to wait. Having found true love at last, she was eager to explore all the delicious sensations he provoked in her while they were still so fresh and tender.

Her heart and her honour were safe in

his keeping. Champagne or no champagne, Sylvie had never been more certain of anything in her life.

Music wafted in through her half-opened window on the mild night air. A faint shimmer of star and lantern light bathed the darkened room, enough for Sylvie to discern vague shapes and shadows.

Her bridegroom nuzzled her neck. "If you change your mind at any time, please tell me and I will stop." He inhaled deeply, as if her scent was the only air that would sustain him. "I swear I will...if it kills me."

Sylvie subsided against him with a wanton chuckle. "Do not expect me to excuse you so easily from your duties as a husband."

With that, she untied her mask and tossed it to the floor. Then she took his hand and led him towards the bed. On the way, she heard the quiver of arrows fall from his Robin Hood costume. He must have removed his mask, too. For when he eased Sylvie onto the cool sheets and began to kiss her again, his upper face was as delightfully naked as the rest of him would soon be.

For a while they reveled in kissing and touching through their clothes, murmuring endearments, not worrying that their knees might buckle when passion swept over them. And sweep it did, with a fluid force as powerful and inevitable as billows on the ocean.

Her lover kicked off his boots, and Sylvie, her slippers. With impatient, fumbling fingers, she tugged at the laces that held his vest closed. Gradually his kisses grew more fevered, stoking the blaze of her desire. His lips strayed lower, pushing aside the light fabric of her Greek chiton bodice with his chin until he had bared her breast for his delectation...and hers.

Sylvie swallowed a little gasp when his lips closed over the crest of her bosom, followed by the first hot swipe of his tongue. She arched herself towards him, her gasp muting into a purr of pleasure. She could feel his lips curve into a smile as he continued to favour her with the delightful worship of his body.

Slipping his hand beneath the hem of her gown, he began to trace the contour of her leg. With every inch his velvet touch ascended, her delight and her need grew, until she wondered how her senses could contain them. When he halted, then began to retreat, only a forceful application of his lips upon hers kept Sylvie from crying out her sharp, sweet yearning.

"I must get out of these clothes!" His hoarse whisper rasped in Sylvie's ear, echoing her own thoughts precisely.

After a brief, frantic struggle to remove their costumes, they subsided back onto the sheets with soft sounds of fulfilment, relishing the contact between their naked bodies, which fairly glowed with mutual desire. Sylvie pushed her lover onto his back, pinning him beneath her, eager to explore and excite him, as he had done to her.

"Enough!" He spoke in a soft, urgent growl at last. "If you keep this up, I will be no more good to you."

"Indeed?" She chuckled. "Is that how it works? I fear I have much to learn about the doings of husbands and wives."

"I have no vast experience myself," he admitted. "Shall we learn together?"

Sylvie wriggled against him, delighting in the feel of his firm-muscled chest against her bosom. "I am prepared to devote countless hours to the pursuit of such vital knowledge."

"And I shall be your willing partner in...study."

Once again he began to kiss and fondle her with untutored prowess born of desire and love for her. As the music of a summer night engulfed them and swept them away, they came together at last in a surge of wild magic that would have been worth a lifetime of waiting and wanting.

The music had long since died away and dawn's rosy light had begun to filter in the window when West's eyes snapped open, roving restlessly while his body lay in breath-bated stillness.

Dear heaven, what had he done?

He'd thought last night had all been a delicious, champagne-sodden dream. Now he stared at Sylvie, her features relaxed in the soft, trusting tranquility of sleep as she nestled beside him in her bed.

Her bed! The spell of their midsummer night tryst shattered into a thousand perilous shards. How might Sylvie look when she opened her lovely eyes and saw *him* in her bed rather than Viscount Allingham? West's newly vulnerable heart quailed at the prospect.

He had been reluctant to coerce Sylvie into wedding him out of duty. Now he had done something far more despicable. He'd made his way into her bed under false pretences, in the guise of another man. Having yielded to his seduction, she would now be forced to wed him to prevent a scandal. If she could ever forgive him the former, West was certain she would hate him for the latter.

Almost as much as he hated himself for abandoning his restraint and his scruples. Last night, somewhere between the rose garden and her bedroom, his befuddled conscience had urged him to doff his mask so Sylvie would know it was he. Caught in the wayward grip of passion, he had ignored his own better judgment.

Now, in the soft, cool light of daybreak, West bitterly repented his impetuous actions.

For a bittersweet moment, he let his gaze brood over Sylvie's naked body, her lithe limbs wrapped in the lazy contentment of sated desire. He wanted her now as much as he had last night.

More, perhaps, for having experienced the rapture of their lovemaking. He could not bear to tarnish the memory of their enchanted night with the aversion he might see in her eyes if he stayed, nor with the kind of bitter recriminations he deserved from her.

Unable to face her until he had some time to marshal his old defences, West eased himself out of Sylvie's bed, gathered up his clothes and stole away.

CHAPTER 8

Sylvie stirred in her sleep when the door of her bedroom closed with faint finality. She made an effort to snuggle deeper into her lover's warm embrace, only to find him gone.

Gone! She pried her eyes open, trying to push aside the muddled fog of sleep and ignore the queasy feeling deep in her stomach.

It had all happened as she remembered, hadn't it? The kiss, the vows, the midnight bliss of lovemaking — they weren't just some romantic dream conjured up by the atmosphere of Lord Daventry's masked ball and the quantity of champagne she'd consumed? She might have been tempted to think so, but for the mild ache of her surrendered virginity and the memory of what potent delight she had found in her lover's arms. That had been beyond the powers of her imagination.

When she glanced about the room,

hoping for some tangible sign, Sylvie spied her lover's black mask lying on the floor with her silver one. She climbed out of bed and picked it up, turning it over and over in her hands.

Why had he stolen away so early, without so much as a kiss of parting?

A little shiver went through her when she imagined them rediscovering the pleasures of the night all over again at sunrise. How much might it add to the experience, to be able to feast her eyes on the firm, masculine beauty of his naked body? To see the flicker of carnal admiration for her in his gaze, muting into the soft glow of devotion. She could picture it all.

Another shiver followed the first, though far less pleasant. Had she made vows of eternal love with the right man? Had the lover she'd welcomed into her bed been the one she'd intended?

In the enchantment of last night, she had been so certain. In the cool, rational light of morning, Sylvie feared she might have made a disastrous mistake. Neither could she trust his feelings for her. If he cared as much as he'd made her believe, surely he would not have departed this morning with neither word nor kiss nor any assurance of his identity.

What a harsh jest Fate might have played on her — teaching her the truth of her feelings only to place her in a situation where she might have to wed a man she could not love. She wanted to burrow under the bedclothes and weep her heart out.

But she did not.

She was a woman now, Sylvie reminded herself. Not a flighty girl who would let starlight fancies blind her to the ripe golden promise of every day. A woman must be willing to strive for what she wanted in life, make firm choices, then live with the consequences and make all she could out of them. Which meant, she must undertake the most difficult task she had ever set herself.

She must talk honestly and intimately with Auberon Westborne and compel him to answer her in kind.

West's courage almost deserted him when he spied Sylvie marching towards him through the orangery of Helmhurst. She had a determined look on her face and in her hand she clutched the black mask he'd worn the previous night. The mask behind which he had hidden to deceive and seduce her.

The moment he'd feared for so long had come at last. In fact, it would be worse than he had feared, for not only would he lose any hope of Sylvie's love, he would also lose her respect and her friendship. He had not treasured those two precious

gifts highly enough.

"West?" Sylvie's face looked pale and there were dusky shadows beneath her eyes. West had never seen her so resolute nor so achingly beautiful.

"Do you know anything about this?" She held out the mask. "I must have the truth now, mind. For the sake of a very long and dear acquaintance."

A dear acquaintance against which he had so despicably transgressed.

West reached for her hand as he sank to his knees. "I would beg your forgiveness, but I fear that would be asking the impossible. I admit I wore that mask last night, and Allingham's costume as well. I'd overheard the two of you talking in the garden the night before and planning to meet."

He did not tell her that Lord Daventry had provided him with the costume. The blame was his for putting it to the use he had.

Before Sylvie could berate him, he rushed on, desperate to make a clean breast of it. "I was a rank scoundrel to deceive you and compromise you as I did last night. My only feeble excuse is that I have loved you so long and, lately, with so little hope."

"Honour will compel us to wed." West kept his eyes cast down, shrinking from the contempt he was sure to see in Sylvie's eyes. He knew what he must do to make amends, though it would condemn him to a lifetime of fresh heartbreak. "I swear I will make no demands on you once we are married and I will allow you every freedom you would enjoy as a single woman."

If that meant the humiliation of watching her flaunt her love affairs under his nose or even letting the children of her lovers bear his name, it was no more than he deserved.

"Auberon Westborne!" Sylvie cried.

She pulled at his hand. Thinking she wished to be released from his touch, West let her go.

To his amazement, Sylvie grasped his hand and pulled him to his feet. "Do you truly believe I would have taken you into my bed last night if I had not known all along it was you?"

"Known?" West shook his head.

This could not be a summer night's dream, for it was morning. A morning suddenly sparkling with golden hope and promise.

"Of course, known!" Sylvie hurled herself into his arms. "How could you think I would accept such a sudden proposal unless I had known my suitor for a very long time, and grown to love him without ever realizing it?"

"You did? You do?" His heart was too full to say more just then, so he let his lips

speak for him...without words.

When at last they drew apart, Sylvie looked deep into his eyes, and West saw the love he had long despaired of finding.

"I will forgive your error in thinking I could give myself to a man I'd just met." She dealt his nose a teasing bat with her forefinger. "If you can forgive my youthful folly in believing I could never fall in love with a man I've known all my life. A man I mean to know a good deal better in the years to come," she added, offering him her lips in earnest of her heart. "A man I mean to love forever."

"Know better," West agreed, savouring a world turned topsy-turvy in the most delightful way. "Love forever."

Deep, long and sweet they kissed, then, discovering a magic that needed no champagne, no rose gardens and no starlight to weave its potent spell around their hearts. ∎

Step back into the sparkling and elegant Regency period and enjoy passion on the high seas with DEBORAH HALE's The Bride Ship. Out in January in Historical Romance™.

Ed Gardener's

If you're blessed with green fingers – or just want to have a go – our favourite landscape gardener Ed has shared his trusty log book for the year.

JANUARY

"If St Paul's be fair and clear, it does betide a happy year" – St Paul's Day being 25th January

Plant deciduous shrubs and trees if ground conditions allow. Crocus, early narcissi and snowdrops will be flowering now.

Recommended plant for January Helleborus (many colours). Plant in containers or borders.

FEBRUARY

"If Candlemas Day be fair and bright, Winter will have another flight, If on Candlemas Day it's showers and rain, Winter is gone will not come again"

Celebrate signs of spring!

With camellias, daphne and heathers all in flower. If you have space grow some vegetables and herbs – very rewarding and helps save the pennies!

Recommended plant for February Camellia. Plant in containers or shrub beds.

MARCH

"March comes in like a lion, goes out like a lamb"

March is potentially the busiest time in the garden. Planting of deciduous trees, shrubs, roses and fruits should be completed this month. Seed sowing of flowers and vegetables under glass. Final prune of roses. Spring flowers, including magnolia, forsythia, kerria, prunus and ribes, are flowering now. Early cut of the lawn may be required!

Log Book

Recommended plant for March
Magnolia stellata. Plant in containers
or shrub beds.

APRIL

"April showers bring forth May flowers"

Many are tempted to plant summer
bedding plants too early – the risk of
frost is still a possibility. Better to wait a
few weeks. It's a good time to plant
evergreen trees, shrubs and climbers –
water as necessary. Top dress lawns,
sow grass seed.
**Recommended plant for
April** Rhododendron.
Plant in containers
or shrub beds.

MAY

**"Don't cast a clout till
May is out"
(Keep your vest on!)**

May brings a taste of
summer but there is still a
risk of late frost.
Keep an eye on local
weather forecasts before
planting out your
summer
bedding
and
hanging
baskets.

Popular cottage garden plants include
delphinium, lupin, hollyhocks and
cornflower.

Recommended plant for May
Fuchsia. For colour all summer long!
Plant in containers or beds.

JUNE

**"Evening red and morning grey
Are the signs of a fine day"**

Prune spring flowering shrubs. All
planters and containers will require
watering throughout the summer.
Try to collect rainwater
wherever possible in water
butts and use bark mulch
and mushroom compost
on beds to contain
moisture.

Recommended plant for June
Cistus (rock rose) for beautiful
summer colour. Plant in containers
and shrub beds.

JULY

**"On St Swithin's Day, if it rains,
For forty days it will remain."**

Dead-head roses, summer prune fruit
trees. Composting, recycling of garden
and kitchen waste is very important
and useful. Compost bins take up little

room and provide a good, natural material for improving soil structure.

Recommended plant for July
Pieris – all-year round colour, you'll be the envy of your neighbours!
Plant in containers or beds.

AUGUST

"If the 24th August is fair and clear Then hope for a prosperous autumn that year"

Brilliant colours of mid-summer this month with bedding plants, Roses, Herbaceous and summer flowering shrubs at their very best.
Keep dead-heading all plants to encourage more flowers.

Recommended plant for August
Rose (old garden roses). Sweetly scented with colourful rosehips in Autumn. Plant wherever you have room.

SEPTEMBER

"September blow soft till the fruit's in the loft"

September in recent years has seen the warm weather continue,

prolonging the colourful show of flowering plants and extending the season for fruit and vegetables. It's a good time to sow grass seed to get established before the colder weather.

Recommended plant for September
Hydrangea. For late summer colour. Plant in containers or shrub beds.

OCTOBER

"When great leaves fall the winter is at hand"

October heralds the autumn colours and leaf fall. It's time to remove summer bedding and replace with winter bedding plants that will provide colour until spring. Pansies and polyanthus are the most popular. Bulbs can be planted now for spring flowering. Roses that have finished flowering can be reduced in height.

Recommended plant for October
Acer palmatum. Vivid autumn colour. Plant in containers or shrub beds.

NOVEMBER

"A fair day in winter is the mother of a storm"

Frosty weather is usual this month. Leaves are still falling and need clearing frequently. If you have space, composting these leaves will give you a valuable – and cheap – material over time for adding to your soil. Vegetable plots will benefit from digging over allowing frost to break down the soil.

Recommended plant for November
Amelanchier. A large spring flowering shrub with autumn cheer.
Plant in containers or shrub beds.

DECEMBER

"A good winter brings a good summer"

A quiet month in the garden (hooray!). Pruning of fruit trees required and the last of the leaves to clear up to add to your compost. Popular plants that lighten up the winter months with their brightly coloured berries include pyracantha, cotoneaster and skimmia.

Recommended plant for December
Wisteria. Climbing shrub for pergolas and walls.

Wisteria

New Year's

Here's a delightful way to welcome

Celebrate on New Year's Day with a festive afternoon Open House! One of the most enjoyable ways to usher in the New Year is with an informal gathering of friends on New Year's Day. By planning ahead, and limiting your menu to a few easy-to-prepare dishes, you can invite dozens of guests and still have time (and energy) to enjoy yourself! Invite your guests to drop in any time between 3:00 pm and 6:00 pm. Some neighbours may come by briefly just for a glass of punch, while your closer friends will probably stay on for the entire party.

Tips so you have as much fun as your guests:

Keep it simple! Entertaining on this scale means that, unless you enjoy spending hours in the kitchen, complicated recipes are out. Jazz up the ordinary. Stick to the foods you know and dress them up for the occasion! For example, you can jazz up a raw-vegetable platter by adding an assortment of unusual dips and salsas—white bean dip, yoghurt-cheese-and-spinach dip or salsa. Or offer something unusual—instead of chilli, serve up taco with grilled chicken.

Order in! If the thought of cooking for a crowd leaves you weak, let your fingers do the walking!

Just dessert! Instead of serving a complete meal, focus on dessert! Hand-held desserts are a good idea. Serve platters of cookies, brownies and cakes. If your friends want to contribute, tell them to bake a batch of their favourite biscuits. A large selection of delicious sweets makes any gathering a success—and your friends will be glad to help out, adding to the fun!

Day Open House!

the New Year with friends and neighbours…

Drink up! You may wish to serve wine or other alcoholic drinks, but consider making a delicious non-alcoholic punch the centrepiece of your drink display. At least some of your guests will appreciate it! If you don't have one in the attic, try to beg or borrow a beautiful punch bowl for the occasion. Freeze a large container of ice ahead of time, and place the ice in the punch bowl. Four bottles of ginger ale make a good basis for your punch, to which you might add cranberry, orange or pineapple juice, and add cut-up fruit and lemon or orange slices. You can't go wrong.

WINEGLASS "Charms"!

Here's a party idea that's festive and practical, too! Place drink charms around the stems of your wineglasses, so your guests can keep track of their glass during the party! Drink charms are popular—and they can be expensive. But they're easy to make! Simply thread plastic or glass beads (or other small items) onto earring wire or a bit of pipe cleaner. Remember, the charms must be different from each other, so guests can tell which glass is theirs.

Ring out the old,
New Year's celebrations

As New Year approaches and you are planning which party to go to and who you'll be singing Auld Lang Syne with – we thought we'd give you some inspiration by taking a look at how the rest of the world sees in the New Year…

In **America** the New Year begins on the east coast. Perhaps that's why the famous ball lowering at Times Square, in New York, has become so popular. The first ball-lowering celebration was held on December 31, 1907. The original ball was made of iron and wood and was decorated with 100 25-watt light bulbs.

Many other New Year's traditions began as religious or folk celebrations. In **Rio de Janeiro**, for example, it's customary to dress in white, to bring good luck and peace during the New Year. After midnight the Cariocas (as the residents of Rio are known) go to the beach, jump seven waves and throw flowers into the sea while making a wish. It is believed that the goddess who protects the sea will make the wish come true.

In **Japan** people make rice cakes… in **Ecuador** they wear masks to drive away bad luck…

Though customs vary around the world, for a happy, healthy year filled with

Ring in the new!
around the world.

In Spain they eat 12 grapes, one with each chime of the clock... and in Germany they serve a platter of doughnuts, one of which is filled with mustard! No matter where you live, the New Year is celebrated with time-honoured traditions!

The Chinese New Year is celebrated in February, and the celebration lasts for two weeks. One ancient tradition involves the making of paper dragons and other fanciful creatures, often cut from red paper and pasted onto windows. The Chinese believe that these paper cuttings will scare away evil spirits, which are unable to get into the house through the decorated windows.

In Thailand the New Year begins on April 13. On this day, Thai people return to their hometowns to pay their respects to parents and grandparents and to ask for good luck. The next morning, children receive blessings from their grandparents, along with some new money—because new things are needed to get a good start in the New Year.

One of the most unusual New Year's traditions takes place in Colombia. It's called "Burning Mr Old Year." The family gathers and makes a big male doll stuffed with old clothes and objects that are associated with sad memories. Then, at midnight, the doll is set on fire. This symbolizes the burning of the past to make way for a happy New Year without bad memories!

what they have in common is the wish peace and good luck. HAPPY NEW YEAR!

From the bestselling author of
Thursdays at Eight

Finding friendship in unexpected places…

Debbie Macomber

The Shop on Blossom Street

finding friendship in unexpected places…

Can you tell from first impressions whether someone could become your closest friend?

Thirty-year-old Lydia has survived cancer twice. Image conscious Jacqueline is in her mid-forties with an empty marriage. High-powered thirty-seven-year-old Carol longs for a baby and is hoping for one last miracle, and Alix, angry and defensive from a tough childhood, needs someone special.

None of these women could ever have guessed how close they would become or where their friendship would lead them.

MIRA

CONNECT IT

Each line in the puzzle below has three clues and three answers. The last letter in the first answer on each line is the first letter of the second answer, and so on. The connecting letter is outlined, giving you the correct number of letters for each answer (the answers in line 1 are 4, 5 and 7 letters). The clues are numbered 1 to 8, with each number containing 3 clues for the 3 answers on the line. But here's the catch! The clues are not in order – so the first clue in Line 1 may (or may not) actually be for the second or third answer in that line. Got it? Good luck!

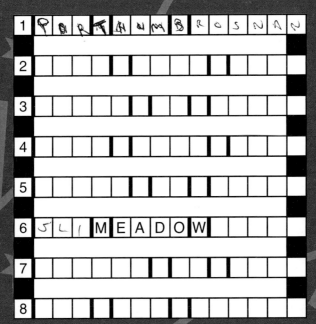

Clues

1. Tom ___, pulled out a plum. 007 star. Dessert wine.
2. Loud. Cake sweetener. Hamlet star.
3. Renovate. Troy star. Subjects.
4. Song. Sleek ship. Another Troy star.
5. Opinion. Coy. Fugitive star.
6. Hudson Hawk star. Slender. Pasture.
7. Hindu philosophy. Another 007 star. Fragrance.
8. Tin Cup star. Another song. Ointment.

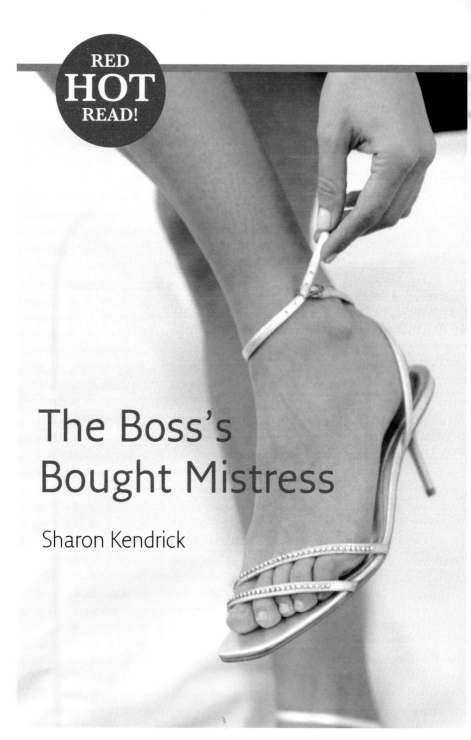

The Boss's Bought Mistress

Sharon Kendrick

"Wrecked!" screamed the caption beneath the photo of a woman being bundled, glassy eyed into the back of a police car.

"*Che cosa cha facenda?*" His black eyes glittering, Giovanni threw down the newspaper and turned to his spin doctor. "Let's hope this is the last of it."

"You've spoken to the police?" asked Lucas.

"*Si*. The lawyers say charges will be dropped if she goes into rehab," Giovanni said grimly. "She's finally accepted that she has a problem. But *Madre di Dio* — it has taken long enough!"

After years of denial, his fragile stepsister had taken the first, tentative step on the road to recovery. But despite the sunshine that streamed through the windows of his beautiful London house, Giovanni couldn't shake off his disquiet.

"But what the hell do I do now?" he questioned, his dark features hardening as he anticipated the troubles ahead. "How do I stop the snappers from camping outside the clinic and bribing patients to sell gossip? My sister needs protecting from the sharks who inhabit her world, and God knows there's nobody else looking out for her."

"We need to kill the story," said Lucas, quietly.

"How?"

"We give the press an even bigger one.

A diversionary tactic."

Giovanni narrowed his eyes. "And what could be bigger than this?"

"You are."

"Explain," Giovanni said tersely.

"They want a story about your fabulously glamorous family."

"And fabulously cursed," echoed Giovanni sardonically. "Don't forget that."

Lucas shrugged. "Drugs are big, but you're one of the world's most eligible bachelors. Your engagement story would wipe everything else off the front page."

"Engagement story?" Giovanni sat down and stretched out his long legs as he studied his spin doctor thoughtfully. "What black arts are you concocting now, Lucas?" he murmured.

"An engagement of convenience," replied the other man smoothly.

In spite of everything, Giovanni gave a short laugh. "Aren't you forgetting something? There's no one who fits the bill. In fact, there's no particular woman in my life." Relationships bored him — and scared the life out of him. He'd spent his early years avoiding the fallout of partnerships, which always seemed flawed and ultimately doomed...

"Which is what would make it such a good story," persisted Lucas. "It would be

145

so out of character."

"I may want to protect my step-sister," said Giovanni grimly, "but there's a limit to what I'm prepared to do."

"No one's asking you to go through with it," placated Lucas. "Just join in with the game, that's all. Buy the ring. Play cat and mouse with the cameras. The press will go wild and by the time they've finished chasing you, Miranda will be clean and sober. We can get her discharged somewhere quiet and you can call the whole thing off."

Giovanni gave a stare that would have intimidated most men. "And who's going to agree to be my wife?" he questioned sarcastically. "Any bright ideas?"

Lucas smiled. "Oh, come on, Giovanni — you practically have to fight them off!"

Giovanni shrugged. It was true. He could have his pick of any woman he wanted — whenever, wherever and however he wanted. If word went out that he was looking for a bride, then they would be lining up around the block. Women flocked to him like ants to jam — attracted to his good looks and legendary sex-appeal, as well as his massive bank account and starry address book.

And therein lay the problem.

He flicked Lucas a questioning look. "And when it's all over? What woman is going to take kindly to being dumped?"

"Not one...unless you tell her the truth first. Number-one rule of spin — don't tell lies; just be sparing with the facts."

"But that would mean trusting them."

"And there isn't anyone...?"

Giovanni gave a brittle smile. A woman he could trust? Were there pots of gold at the ends of rainbows? His teenage years had been spent watching avaricious women bleed his father's fortune dry. And when Giovanni was just sixteen, one of the women had even come to his room late at night — astonished when the rugged youth had turned down her offer of sex.

"No," he answered shortly. "There isn't."

The silence that followed was splintered by a smart, seasoned rap on the door.

Giovanni stretched and yawned. "Yes, come in," he said, without bothering to turn round.

The woman who pushed the tea trolley into the elegant drawing room was just short of her thirtieth birthday and didn't really have a job description.

In the days when even the aristocracy had the bare minimum of people working for them, Misty Carmichael had a number of skills at her disposal. She was able to cook, clean and serve food and sometimes she was called on to do all three in rapid succession.

She looked across at her not-quite-Lord, but certainly her master — the arrogant but drop-dead-gorgeous Giovanni Cerruti. In four years of working for him, she had tried not to love him, or to react to him as a woman. It hadn't been easy and it still wasn't, but Giovanni had helped by managing to make her feel as if she was invisible.

"Coffee?" she asked.

"Please," said Giovanni absently. "Well, I'll give your idea some thought, Lucas."

But Lucas did not reply. He was watching the woman as she poured coffee — the steam making her pale cheeks grow pink.

Misty offered a plate of tiny macaroons, thinking how strained Giovanni looked. "Would you like a biscuit?"

"No, I wouldn't," said Giovanni impatiently. "You know I never eat between meals."

Irritated, he glanced over at Lucas. Why the hell was he staring at Misty like that? He followed the direction of his spin-doctor's eyes and for the first time noticed that Misty's checked working dress was pulling very tightly across her bottom. Two tight globes thrusting against the man-made fibre. It was as though he was seeing her for the very first time and inexplicably, a nerve began to work in his cheek.

Misty glared at them both. What were they staring at? Had her hair suddenly turned green? "Will that be all?"

"Er, yes. Thank you."

Lucas turned to Giovanni, who was still staring at Misty's retreating bottom.

"Why not her?" he questioned simply once she had gone.

"Her?" Giovanni flared his haughty nostrils, and laughed. "Are you honestly suggesting I get engaged to one of the staff?"

CHAPTER TWO

"What's wrong with getting engaged to a member of your staff?"

Giovanni's jet black eyes narrowed as he stared at his spin doctor. "*Madre di Dio!* You are proposing that I ask Misty Carmichael? Are you crazy, Lucas? She serves the meals!"

"That could be useful," said Lucas.

"And she is a single mother!" Giovanni exclaimed.

"So?"

"So I have my reputation to think about!"

Lucas shook his head. "But this is a bogus engagement, remember? Designed to take the heat off your sister's spell in rehab. The more unsuitable the candidate, the more press coverage it will get. Think about it, Giovanni."

Giovanni did, his arrogant lips curving with distaste. "She is plain..." he added disparagingly.

From the other side of the door, Misty froze. She had just crept back to hear the tail end of Giovanni's conversation.

Plain?

She bit her lip and blinked rapidly. Plain?

So it was true what they said — that eavesdroppers never hear anything good about themselves. And how! Listening in to her employer's conversation wasn't her usual pastime, but who could blame her on this occasion?

The peculiar way that Giovanni and his new spin doctor had been staring at her had been enough to make her feel concerned, and with good cause, she now recognised.

"So ring and ask her," came Lucas's voice from the other side of the door.

Ask her what, she wondered?

Hurriedly, Misty pushed the tea trolley back into the kitchen. There was only a second to check her appearance in the mirror before the bell began to summon her back again.

Frizzy hair, flushed cheeks and PMS making her tummy look fat. She winced. Plain indeed. Why feel insulted by Giovanni's description of her when it was nothing but the truth?

She rapped on the door and walked into the spotlight of Giovanni's blazing ebony stare which, unusually, was fixed unwaveringly on her.

"I want you to do me a favour, Misty,"

he said, his velvety voice tinged with his faint Italian accent.

Perplexed by his tone, Misty clasped her hands together at her waist. "M-more cake?" she asked stupidly.

Giovanni gave an impatient click of his tongue. On many levels, he and his housekeeper understood each other perfectly. She knew his likes and dislikes. When to keep quiet and when to speak. Unusually, he felt he could be himself around Misty, but her question about cake drove home the great gulf between them.

How the hell did he go about asking her something like this? Especially with his enigmatic spin doctor looking on...

"You can leave us now, Lucas," he ordered.

"Sure."

Misty allowed herself a smug moment as Lucas left the room — he wasn't so high-and-mighty now, was he? Dismissed like a servant himself!

"Sit down," said Giovanni.

Misty was tempted, but she resisted. Something told her she needed all her wits about her, and flopping down onto one of those priceless brocade chairs in her working uniform would surely unsettle her even more.

Especially with Giovanni's long body dominating her line of vision with those strong, muscular legs and the powerful jut of his pelvis. She felt an unwanted prickle of excitement in her breasts, and hastily crossed her arms. "I'm fine as I am."

Giovanni's eyes narrowed thoughtfully as he watched her. The unconscious way she had covered her breasts with her arms told him everything. So she wasn't immune to him — but there again, what woman was? Funny he'd never noticed it before.

And when he stopped to think about it, mightn't her inferior status actually work to his advantage? Because if the woman he involved in his scheme was beautiful and his equal, he might be lured into making love to her — complicating matters more than they needed to be. Whereas there would be zero temptation from this pleasant but very ordinary looking woman...

Then he remembered her pert bottom thrusting against the check material of her uniform and once again, he felt the heat to his groin. Damn Lucas for drawing his attention to it!

"I want you to pretend to be my fiancée," he said huskily.

There was a momentary, pin-drop silence.

"Is this some kind of joke?" she demanded.

"No, Misty..." It occurred to him how rarely he had ever used her name before.

And what a strange name it was. "No. I am being deadly serious."

"Why?" she shot out.

Giovanni expelled an impatient sigh. "I know it must sound bizarre — and it is bizarre. But I need to take the attention off my sister. You know she's been admitted to a clinic?"

"Yes."

"It's just to give the press something bigger to get their teeth into. You know how dangerous they can be. They are sharks," he finished.

But he had no qualms in throwing her to them! Hiding her hurt, Misty stared at him. "What would I have to do?"

Giovanni relaxed. Perhaps this was going to be easier than he had imagined! "Very little," he murmured. "You would wear my ring, of course. Appear by my side in public." His mouth curved into a half smile. "And perhaps you could be persuaded to hold my hand and gaze up at me with suitable adoration from time to time?"

Oh, but he must think she was born yesterday! That mocking tone didn't fool her — not for a moment. He was used to adoration by the bucket-load, and no doubt expected plain Misty Carmichael to shovel on a whole heap more.

So what are you going to do about it?

she asked herself. Let him trample all over you with his handmade Italian shoes?

People like you don't matter to men like him. Remember that.

Misty drew a deep breath. "And what's in it for me?"

Momentarily, Giovanni felt wrong-footed. And oddly disappointed. Had he thought she might agree to the plan out of some misdirected sense of loyalty? Well, that just showed how wrong he could be. His mouth thinned into a cynical smile. She was no different from anyone else.

"You will obviously be paid," he said tightly, his eyes boring into her.

Misty stared at him, her flippant tone disguising the sudden disquiet she felt. "You may not be able to afford me."

His eyes hardened and so did his voice. "Oh, I can afford anyone, Misty," he said coolly. His mouth didn't say it, but his eyes did.

Especially you.

CHAPTER THREE

Misty forced herself not to react to the dark flash of contempt in Giovanni's eyes when she mentioned money. Part of her wished that she'd just kept her mouth shut — and yet what did he expect? That she would go through the hassle of pretending to be his fiancée just for the love of the idea?

Or the love of him?

"So what's your answer, Misty?" he questioned softly. "Or do you want to negotiate your price first?"

Misty shook her head. "You've never been anything other than generous. How long would this pretence have to last?"

"As long as it takes for my sister to clean up her act and get discharged," he said grimly. "Two weeks? Maybe three? Could you bear being in close proximity to me for that long?"

Misty swallowed. Didn't they say be careful of what you wish for, because it can come true? Well, now it had. The man she had worshipped from afar for so long was soon to slip a sparkler on her finger, just like she'd always dreamed.

Only the reality would be as insubstantial as her dreams.

An outsider might have said that she was crazy to want him — but who could blame her? Hadn't he rescued her and given a home to her and her infant son?

The morning she had been interviewed by him, he was wearing a dark business suit and was running late, and frankly she had been surprised that a man so obviously rich and powerful was vetting a would-be housekeeper.

"Security is my concern," he had growled, as if reading her thoughts. "That and loyalty — of which I demand one hundred percent from my staff. Can you deliver that, Ms Carmichael?"

Misty's teeth had just stopped chattering, and she was so glad to be out of the cold and the rain that all she could do was nod her head. And to be honest, she was so desperate for a job that provided accommodation that she would have agreed to dance naked in the middle of the rain-washed street if he'd asked her to.

"Y-yes, sir," she managed.

"You don't have to call me sir," he said, almost gently. "Giovanni is fine." His eyes had narrowed as they raked over her hollow cheeks and her thin coat and cheap shoes. "How long since you ate a decent meal?" he demanded.

Misty's stomach turned over and for a moment she really thought she might faint from hunger. But it was pointless getting all fed and settled — not if she wasn't going to be allowed to stay...

"I have a baby," she said fiercely.

Giovanni stifled a groan. Get rid of her. Now.

"Will that be a problem?" Misty persisted.

He opened his mouth to say yes, but something in her expression stopped him.

A sudden look of defiance had injected her defeated air with something approaching courage — transforming her half-starved frame into a feisty little fighter.

But Giovanni knew that babies born to single mothers tended to have bad or sad histories.

"How old?"

"Dominic is ten months."

He ignored the tone of maternal pride. "And what about the father?"

"He's..." Misty bit her lip. "He's no longer on the scene."

"But maybe he wants to be. What's to say he isn't going to turn up here, banging on the door? Demanding to see his son? Demanding to see you?"

The pain on Misty's face came from the reminder that she had been such an appalling judge of character. "No," she said quietly. "He won't come round. He didn't want to know about the baby."

"You're still in love with him?"

Misty shook her head. "No," she whispered. She had been taken in by a heartless, serial seducer. It had not been love — it had been poor judgment.

And then Giovanni saw how close to breaking point she was and wondered how he could have been quite so brutal. Swearing softly, he pushed her down into a chair.

"Where is...Dominic now?"

151

"He's downstairs being looked after by the cook."

Madre di Dio but he had saddled himself with the strayest of all cats! Bringing her litter with her and depositing it in his kitchen!

But something of the baby's plight reminded him of his own childhood — of all the disruption and fighting following his parents' bitter divorce.

At that moment he'd decided to take charge and soon had Misty eating a large bowl of soup and the baby asleep by the range. Somehow — magically — a proper cot and high chair were delivered that same evening and put upstairs in the two rooms he'd allotted them at the top of his large house.

What woman in the world wouldn't have loved a man who had done that for her? Particularly as Dominic had thrived there, like a carefully tended plant.

The house was situated in the heart of London and Giovanni insisted that nursery fees were part of her salary — Misty knew that she could never have afforded them herself. And when it had been time for Dominic to start school, Giovanni had made sure there was an allowance for his uniform. Misty's pride had been fierce when she saw him in his little blue-and-grey uniform, a cap sitting atop the thick thatch of hair.

Except that the fairy-tale had stopped

there. Things had settled down and Giovanni had taken a step back and become nothing more than her boss.

Had she been hoping for more?

Yes, yes, yes! Of course she had — no matter how many times she had tried to tell herself that he never even looked at her as a woman. And why would he look at a woman like her? Giovanni knew no more about her than he had on the day she came looking for a job.

So maybe this mad scheme made sense. Perhaps it was just what Misty needed to jolt her out of her complacency and her rut.

"You still haven't given me your answer," said Giovanni softly.

"But what will I tell Dominic?" Misty asked him, biting her lip.

CHAPTER FOUR

Giovanni stared at Misty. "What does it matter what you tell your son?" he demanded.

Misty gave a gulp of disbelief. "He's five years old! Don't you have *any* idea what five-year-old boys are like?"

"Oddly enough, no," he answered repressively.

"Yet presumably you were once one yourself?"

Giovanni leapt on the word like a dog on a bone. "What do you mean *presumably*?"

Misty bit back her instinctive retort — that emotionally he was so cold, someone might have assembled him in a laboratory! "Then surely you can remember back to the insecurities of a little boy?"

"I don't remember having any," he said slowly, because the question was so unlike any he was ever asked that it didn't occur to him to answer it anything but truthfully.

And Misty could believe that. "Did you go to school in England?" she asked curiously, aware that he had let his guard down and wanting to peep through this rare chink in his armour.

He shook his dark head. "I started school in Italy — a tiny school in the mountains — close to my grandmother's house."

It was all too easy to picture what the powerful billionaire must have been like as a little boy. The ebony hair and solemn dark eyes...and perhaps the beginnings of the elusive smile that would later capitvate legions of women.

"Is that where you lived?"

"I was staying there," he answered tightly.

"And then where?" persisted Misty tentatively, recognizing that she'd learnt more about him in the past ten minutes than she had in four years.

Giovanni stilled. He didn't revisit the past too often but it seemed that when you started down that road, it gathered momentum and the memories just kept flooding in.

"Later I switched between England and Paris, then universities in the States. That's the beauty of having parents from different countries — you get a varied education, even if they hate each other."

She heard the pain in his voice, and it surprised her.

Or did you think that Giovanni's power and privilege protected him from pain? mocked an inner voice in her head.

"Anyway," he drawled, his whole demeanour changing as he met her eyes. "Fascinating as this is, I'm still not sure what the problem is about telling Dominic. Why tell him anything?"

"Do you think he lives in a bubble, and that the parents of his classmates don't read the papers?" She drew her chin up with sudden determination. "Do you have any idea of what the real world's like?"

Giovanni smiled. She was animated. Feisty. Suddenly, he was taken back to the night she arrived, like a stray cat with her litter. "Why don't you tell me?" he questioned softly.

Should she? Well, why not? She had nothing to lose. "Other women at the school try to befriend me because I work for you."

Giovanni's eyes narrowed. "Why would they do that?"

"Oh, Gio — don't be dense!"

153

No one had called him Gio for years — and no one had ever called him dense. "Why?" he repeated silkily.

"Because you're sexy, rich and single and they..." Her voice trembled. "They want you!"

There was a pin-drop silence.

"They want me?" he repeated incredulously.

"I shouldn't have said that," she moaned.

But Giovanni didn't appear to be listening. "Do you think that, too?"

"Wh-what?"

He moved closer — close enough for the pale blue from her startled eyes to wash over him. "That I'm sexy?"

His sheer magnetism alone was enough to imprison her, but then his arm snaked out to wrap itself around the narrow indentation of her waist and made the prison physical. The kind of prison you'd want to escape from...but she wanted to stay there forever.

"W-what are you doing?" she stammered out.

He wasn't sure. The only thing he was sure of was that the pump of blood to his groin was making his head spin. He shook it in disbelief.

He had chosen Misty Carmichael to play this role precisely because she was unsuitable as his fiancée. So what was he doing coming on to her like it was real? Like a man who hadn't had sex in a long time?

Giovanni frowned and abruptly let her go.

"I shouldn't have done that," he grated.

Misty prayed for the thundering in her heart to subside. "It was only a hand on my waist," she said lightly, through parched lips. But it had been more than that — he knew it, and she knew it. And by playing it down, mightn't he think that she turned on for any man that quickly?

"So will Dominic be disappointed that I'm not really going to be his new step-daddy?" he queried coolly.

"Hardly." She gave a thin smile. "I just don't want to spin him any lies, that's all."

"How very admirable," he commented.

She met his mocking look with one of her own. "I may not have made a success of many areas of my life," she said quietly, "but I have always tried to be a good mother."

Her soft dignity made him feel as if he had attempted to score a cheap point and Giovanni felt even more unsettled. What was going on? How come she was making him feel all this stuff?

"Is there nowhere he can go, so as not to disrupt him too much?"

Misty thought about it for a bit. "I guess he could go and stay with his godmother in Cornwall."

"And you can tell him that Mummy's going to earn enough money to take him on a lovely holiday!"

Maybe Giovanni was trying to be kind, but Misty winced. He made her sound like some kind of hooker.

He was staring at her bare face and frizzy hair. "And while we're at it," he drawled, "you're going to need an urgent makeover. Because no one will ever believe I want to marry you, looking like that."

CHAPTER FIVE

"Nervous?" Giovanni murmured.

Misty turned to look at him, scarcely able to believe this was happening — and to her! That the man at her side just happened to be Giovanni Cerruti, the sexy Italian who was one of the richest men on the planet.

And as far as the world was concerned, she was his fiancée!

"Surprisingly, I'm getting used to it," she mused. "Though I've never been to a ball before."

Giovanni gave a half smile. He had never met a woman who told the truth quite like Misty. This week at dinner, she had charmed a hard-bitten politician by asking him to show her how to eat an oyster! "Most women wouldn't admit to that," he observed softly.

She tilted her head to one side. "At least now you know I have an excuse if I let you down in public!"

"You won't let me down, Misty. I'm confident of that." He drifted his eyes over her. Slowly.

"Gio...."

"Mmm?"

His black eyes were suddenly soft, and sweet — like dark treacle. She wanted to say don't flirt with me. Except that wouldn't be true. She liked it, just like she liked him. Too much.

Oh, why had she failed to take her stupid feelings into account when she'd agreed to go along with this sham engagement? And how did she stop wanting make-believe to be real and wondering what it would be like when it was over?

"Do I...do I look okay?"

"Are you fishing for compliments?" he murmured.

"No. Genuinely seeking reassurance before you parade me past the massed

155

banks of press photographers waiting outside and then on to meet the most glittering society in London. Oddly enough, it isn't a situation I find myself in very often."

He wondered if he was always this insensitive. But he didn't usually take a woman's feelings into account — he didn't usually have to. It was all very confusing, and looking at her was confusing him even more. Because her appearance was so different since the makeover that Lucas had organized. She didn't look like Misty, anymore. She looked...

Gone was the frizzy hair, which he had only ever seen tied back in a ponytail. Now the curls were glossy and touched with blond kisses.

Gone was her unflattering uniform and the off-duty jeans he sometimes saw her in. Instead, a silver sheath of a dress clung like syrup to the ripe curves of her body.

But it was her eyes that threw him most. How come he'd never noticed those before? That they were the color of bluebells, which had been left out in the rain too long?

He swallowed. If this was any other woman, he'd have kissed her into compliance by now. But because it was Misty, he knew that intimacy had to be out of bounds. Intimacy?

Surely he meant sex?

"*Si*," he agreed huskily, his spinning thoughts making him slip into his mother tongue. "You look...okay. And now...you are ready?"

Misty nodded. "Yes."

Placing a guiding arm on her shoulders, he pushed open the front door and Misty was transfixed by the force of blinding blue flashing lights that made the nighttime day. She could hear the click of the shutters like a million demented crickets, while the usual insulting questions were shouted at them like hecklers from a crowd.

"Hey, Giovanni — what made you fall for her?"

"Is this a real-life Cinderella story, Giovanni?"

"She isn't your usual type, is she, Giovanni?"

"How does it feel to go downmarket?"

He felt her tense. "Smile," he urged softly, the arm around her tightening protectively. "And keep walking."

With his touch seeming to be the only safe haven in this sea of confusion, Misty pulled her mouth into a kind of rictus as she climbed into the back of the waiting limousine. Giovanni slid in beside her.

"Are you okay?" he asked quickly. "They said some pretty hurtful things."

"I'm getting used to them," she admitted. "But how do you bear it?"

"What?"

"All that!" She waved her hand at the camera lenses, which were pressed against the car windows like alien eyes as it drew away. "Stupid, unnecessary fuss!"

"But press interest goes with the territory," he defended.

"I wonder," she answered softly.

"What's that supposed to mean?"

Misty leaned back against the soft leather seat. "Well, I know that Lucas must have tipped them off tonight, and that's fine because it's all part of the agenda to take the heat off your step-sister. But you're no stranger to the papers yourself, are you? There's always snatched photos of you in the gossip columns."

Instinctively, he bristled against the implied criticism.

"You don't approve?"

Misty thought about it. "It's not for me to approve or disapprove. You're a millionaire many times over — a shining success in the business world," she mused. "I just wonder why you bother employing a spin doctor, that's all."

"Because I have to go out and eat! And I take trips to the theatre!" he declared. "Or are you suggesting I live the life of a hermit? It's better for me to use a spin doctor to manipulate what gets written about me than to leave myself to the mercy of the hacks!"

"Then you're just playing the same

game," she said serenely, though she hadn't thought about it like that before. "And you can't complain when it doesn't go according to your plans."

This was unbelievable! The opinionated little minx was making him sound like some kind of control freak!

And isn't she right?

"I hired you to play my fiancée," he grated. "Not some kind of amateur shrink!"

Misty opened her mouth to object that he *had* asked her opinion, then shut it again. This was not a relationship and it was not equal. He was paying for her company and nothing more. She could see the blazing lights outside the ballroom and yet more waiting cameras. And suddenly, all her nerves vanished.

"You're the boss," she said demurely.

In the half light Giovanni glowered. "*Si, cara*," he grated. "I am." And with that he pulled her into his arms and began to kiss her.

CHAPTER SIX

Giovanni's mouth moved expertly over Misty's, teasing her lips apart while he reached down to circle his thumb over one nipple with exquisite precision. Misty jerked beneath his touch as a long-forgotten arrow of desire shot through her — the memory of pleasure almost too much to bear.

"Gio..." she groaned. And suddenly her hands were beneath his dinner jacket and clawing frantically at the silk of his shirt. "Oh, Gio."

Sweet heaven, but she was hot! Instinctively, Giovanni touched his finger to the fork between her legs, watching her squirm, wanting to tear the dress from her body and to...

"*Dio*, but you are beautiful," he said brokenly.

They were the words that broke the spell. Through the clamour of her starved senses, Misty became dimly aware that the car was pulling to a halt. She tore her mouth away from his, fury lighting her eyes as she looked at his flushed face.

"Oh...my...God," she moaned in disbelief. "How stupid of me! That would have made the most marvellous photo opportunity, wouldn't it?"

"Opportunity had nothing to do with it!" he snapped.

"No?" She straightened her dress and then her hair and gave him an icy look. He'd never looked at her twice in the four years she'd been working with him! "Just overcome with passion, were you?"

"*Si, cara* — I was. Very much so. I still am, if you must know." He saw her mutinous expression and his voice deepened into a sultry whisper. "You must realize how beautiful you look tonight."

But it wasn't really her, was it? It was borrowed, expensive clothes and a chic makeover — and just like Cinderella, she would be back from riches to rags in no time. "It's just an illusion," she said tartly as she climbed out of the car. "Fine feathers make a fine bird!"

But Giovanni breathed a sigh of relief to see her heading for the ballroom. After pouncing on her like that, he wouldn't have blamed her if she'd told him she wanted to go straight back home.

And in truth, wouldn't part of him have approved? So that he could have gone with her...and they could have ended up making love?

Or would they?

For the first time in his life, he wasn't sure that he could get a woman into his bed. She was an unknown factor in more ways than one. A surprisingly thoughtful and articulate woman who had transformed herself, who could give as good as she got.

Just who was the real Misty Carmichael?

He caught up with her, bemused by the glances of the other guests as he ran after her. "Drink?"

"Champagne, please."

He took two glasses from a passing tray. "A woman who knows her mind," he observed.

"It's nice to be on the other side of the tray for once," she answered lightly. "And

please don't patronise me."

Giovanni frowned. "I wouldn't dream of patronisng you."

"Wouldn't you?" Misty questioned wryly.

People clustered round, wanting Giovanni to introduce his fiancée to them. There were business colleagues, aristocratic friends of his parents and more than a few ex and would-be girlfriends who'd clearly had their noses put out of joint.

But Misty was charm personified, shaking hands and smiling until her face ached. Until Giovanni put a firm and proprietorial hand at the small of her back.

"Dance with me."

Enjoying herself hugely, Misty turned to him, her eyes sparkling. "That sounds more like an order."

"I suppose that's how he's used to talking to you," shrilled an over-thin brunette beside her.

Misty didn't miss a beat. "I know," she smiled. "But the masterful touch is terribly attractive, don't you think?"

Giovanni raised his eyebrows as he pulled her onto the dance floor and into his arms. "She's a bitch," he murmured. "But you seemed to cope."

"Why, thank you."

"You're a fast learner, Misty Carmichael," he observed softly.

She dazzled him with a smile, which hid her heartbreak that this was such a game. "That's what you're paying me for, isn't it?"

He wanted to tell her to stop reminding him that this was a business arrangement — but why should he do that? It was exactly that. And maybe he should get his money's worth...

He pulled her against him and her pale blue eyes widened as she felt the tension and unmistakable heat of his body.

"Stop it, Gio," she whispered.

Deliberately, he circled his hips against hers. "Stop what?" he questioned innocently. "We're only dancing."

"We're not," she said weakly. "You know we're not." And her head tipped like an over-heavy flowerhead to rest on his shoulder.

He pulled her even closer so that he could feel the tightening of her breasts, and he placed his mouth next to her ear. "I want you, Misty Carmichael."

She should have told him to go to hell.

"And you want me just as much," he continued inexorably. "I can feel it in your body. If I threw caution to the wind and kissed you, then I'd be able to taste it, too."

"Gio —"

"What?" he questioned, heady now with the sense of sexual power.

"This is...inappropriate."

But never had he felt such a delicious sense of excitement. Could that be because it was so inappropriate, he wondered? Or because he was still by no means certain that he could have her?

How — given his comprehensive knowledge of the opposite sex — could he ensure that Misty Carmichael would be his tonight? What did every woman in the world fall for?

Tenderness.

Unseen, he smiled as he touched his lips to her bare shoulder, and slowly kissed his way all up her neck until he felt her shudder with unspoken surrender.

"Shall we stay or shall we go?" he questioned.

Misty wasn't some naïve virgin — she knew exactly what that question meant. The sexual chemistry fizzing between them wasn't in any doubt — just her own reaction to it. And his.

But if a man kissed a woman as sweetly as Gio had just done, then surely he didn't just see her as a sexual trophy?

Weak with longing, she nodded.

"Yes, let's go now," she whispered.

CHAPTER SEVEN

Giovanni slid down the zipper of Misty's dress and it pooled to her feet in a silver puddle.

"Oh," she gasped, as he touched her between the legs. "Gio...please!"

"Please what, *cara*?" he gasped back, his mouth roaming greedily over her lace-covered nipple like a man who couldn't wait. But he couldn't wait! And his urgency was as unexpected as it was exciting — if only it wasn't so damned inexplicable.

"Please...that?"

"Yes!"

"And that?"

Oh, yes. In the dimly lit hallway of Giovanni's large house, Misty was torn between hopes and dreams and fears. She wanted to beg her boss to be understanding. And slow — as if he really wanted this and had given it careful thought.

"Shouldn't we go upstairs?" she whispered.

"Why not do it here first?" he questioned. "None of the staff will disturb us."

It was a joke about her status as his housekeeper, but it touched a sensitive nerve. And then Giovanni was touching an even more sensitive nerve — sliding her panties down, his finger alighting on the very centre of her womanhood with aching precision.

"Do you like that, too?"

"Y-yes."

"Touch me," he commanded silkily.

Tentatively, she felt the rock-hard ridge of him, her own pleasure increasing as he shuddered beneath her rhythmical stroking. "Do you like that?" she asked nervously.

"Do I like it?" In a minute he would burst. "Unzip me!" he rasped.

She wanted it to be like the million romantic fantasies she'd ever had about him. But she could see it wasn't going to happen that way. Swift and perfunctory wasn't what she would have chosen, but how could she refuse him when she had wanted him for so long?

Sliding his zipper down, she whispered her fingertips over the hard edge of him, praying that she would not disappoint. Would he guess how inexperienced she was? "Tell me what you like," she said. "What you want me to do."

"Just that. Oh..." he breathed on a note of wonder, taken aback by her gentleness and her generosity. He raised his dark head and stared down at her and frowned. Was that doubt clouding her eyes?

"*Dio*! You are not on duty now! Relax, Misty — for tonight we are equals."

But only for tonight, she reminded herself, and Giovanni did not know the half of it. She moved restlessly in his arms as he kissed her, until he suddenly tore his mouth away, scooped her up and began to

161

carry her upstairs.

Misty's eyes snapped open. "Where are you taking me?"

"To bed."

"But I thought you said..."

"I know what I said," he returned fiercely. "And I have changed my mind."

"Just like that," she said weakly. Yet even while she rejoiced at his decision, it only emphasised the fact that he was the master — calling all the shots.

He undressed them both, acquainting himself with every curve and shadow of her lush body until he could feel her relaxing beneath his fingers.

Misty bit her lip as he moved his dark and golden body over her — her emotions so churned up that she was unable to stop them from spilling out. "You are just so beautiful," she breathed.

Giovanni stilled. Most women played games. They held their feelings back in some kind of sexual power play, but not Misty. Her honesty took his breath away...and yet there was something about her naïvety that disturbed him.

"There's still time to change your mind, Misty. Do you want me to stop? Now, before it's too late?"

"Stop?" She curved her hands possessively over his buttocks, shaking her long hair so that it shimmered against his bare chest. "No, I don't want you to stop."

"Sure?"

"Certain."

"Then I can't wait any longer. I'm going to make love to you, Misty Carmichael. Right now..." And with that, he thrust deep inside her. "Oh, you're so hot," he whispered. "And very, very wet."

His words turned her on even more, and Misty melted. Her body felt suffused with heat and the knowledge that Gio was joined so intimately with her.

His lips and his hands were everywhere, touching her in places where she had never been touched — exciting and cajoling her as she felt the tension building and building.

"That's w-wonderful," she said brokenly, as something she didn't quite believe began to tantalize her. Like a blurred picture at last clicking into focus. "Please don't stop."

He gave an odd kind of laugh. "Are you kidding?"

And then it happened — wave upon wave of it rocking her into a brand-new and rainbow-hued dimension. Misty dug her nails into his arms and began to cry out her pleasure as she felt him shudder out his own fulfilment. Then the tears began to fall, even though she tried to stop them.

Giovanni frowned as he felt their wetness on his shoulder. "Misty? Why the hell are you crying?"

She opened her eyes. "B-because that's never happened to me before."

He felt a chill of foreboding. "What hasn't?"

"An...orgasm," she said softly. "I've never had one before."

"How come?" he snapped.

"Because Dominic's father was...well, selfish, I suppose."

"But there must have been other men."

"No."

"You mean that he was your only lover?" he questioned incredulously.

"Until now." She sighed. "Oh, Gio. It was incredible. You were incredible."

Ice-cold dread now crept over him. What the hell had he done? Had sex with a woman who was light years away from him in terms of experience — a woman naïve enough to start mistaking sexual pleasure for something deeper.

And she was wearing his ring! True, it was nothing but a plot to fool the press, but would Misty now conveniently forget that?

And if that was the case then how the hell was he going to get rid of her? Swiftly he withdrew, avoiding her flushed face by turning to face the wall and yawning.

"Would you mind going back to your own room now?" he drawled. "I have a

meeting in the morning and I really need to get some sleep."

CHAPTER EIGHT

Misty could scarcely believe what Giovanni was saying. On trembling legs, she climbed out of bed and stared down at the naked body of her employer with disbelief — knowing that she had behaved no better than a whore.

Only now he was dismissing her like the servant she really was...

"Leave?" she echoed, curving her lip with pride — which wasn't easy when she was gathering up her clothes scattered all over his bedroom, and remembering that her dress was downstairs where it had fallen. "Believe me, nothing will give me greater pleasure!"

Giovanni was beginning to have second thoughts, for she looked magnificent when she was angry. "Nothing at all?" he teased. "I must be losing my touch."

"Don't be cheap," she hissed.

"I may be many things, but I'm not cheap, Misty."

So he was even using this opportunity to rub in the fact that he was paying for her time. "That's a matter of opinion."

Giovanni saw the hurt and the anger, which chased away the rosy flush of sexual fulfillment. And as his body stirred, he began to wonder if he had acted too hastily.

"Well, if you promise to let me sleep, then maybe I'll let you stay here, after all," he drawled, patting the space on the bed beside him and glinting her a look that had a guaranteed 100 percent success rate.

She stared at him in disbelief, realizing that he was serious. "I'd rather sleep on a bed of nails than get back into bed with you!" she spat as she pulled her panties back on. "You can go to hell — you arrogant bastard."

It wasn't the first time that a woman had expressed similar sentiments, but to see Misty do it was unreal. She'd insulted him when he was used to her unswerving loyalty. Misty — steadfast and loyal Misty. Up until a little while ago, he had seen her purely in the role of domestic helper. A stereotype.

But now the real woman had stepped out from behind it. He watched her trying to hook her bra up. And how.

"Can I help?"

"Don't tempt me," she warned.

"I thought I just did."

She composed her face into a withering look he had never seen before.

"Yes, you did, Giovanni — but fortunately I'm grown up enough to learn from my mistakes. And that one must count as my all-time biggest."

And with that, she flounced out of his bedroom and ran to her own at the far end of the house — in the servants quarters, she thought bitterly — where she spent a sleepless night trying to decide where she should go from here.

The following morning, Giovanni paced the house like a caged tiger, and when Misty appeared he searched her face for clues.

"Have you forgiven me?" he questioned softly, but just the sight of her was beginning to make him ache again.

Misty had spent the night deciding how to play this and she was going to play it cool. She couldn't go back to how it had been, which meant she had to go forward. She just wasn't sure where that was going to take her.

"I hadn't really given it a lot of thought."

"Liar," he taunted softly. "Bet you've been awake all night longing for me to do this..."

The finger that brushed slowly over her lips was enough to make her tremble, but Misty jerked her mouth away. "Don't touch me."

His eyes narrowed. "You mean you're backing out of our deal?"

"No." What a cold and calculating man he was. "I'm keeping to my side of it , and I'd appreciate if you kept to yours. I'll continue to be your 'fiancée' until Miranda's out of rehab — I'm just taking sex out of the equation, that's all. But since sex was never supposed to be part of the deal, that shouldn't be a problem, should it?"

"No problem?" he echoed incredulously. "Are you kidding?"

She saw frustration darken his eyes and knew a moment of pure triumph before her traitorous body began to ache for him. Ruthlessly, she suppressed it.

"Not in the slightest." She gave a prim smile. "We'll carry on pretending to be in love, only without any physical complications."

His eyes glittered a challenge. "Want to bet?"

And Misty knew that even if the attempt half killed her, she would resist him. She had to protect herself. She *had* to. "I'm not a betting woman," she snapped.

The front door slammed and Lucas walked in with a stack of newspapers.

"What is it?" asked Giovanni impatiently.

Lucas put the papers down. "This morning's are the best yet! Take a look at these."

Misty stilled, astonished to see herself plastered across the front pages of all the tabloids.

"Good grief," she breathed. "Is that really me?"

Giovanni moved behind her to look over her shoulder.

"It really is," he murmured, wanting to lift the curtain of curls and kiss her neck again.

Misty stared. The photos must have been taken when they were leaving the ball because they both looked flushed and bright-eyed with sexual excitement. Giovanni's arm was locked around her waist and her nipples looked as though someone had splashed them with cold water. Misty blushed.

"And the craziest thing is," Lucas was saying, "that you really look as though you're in love. Great acting, I must say."

But it was apparent the look in Giovanni's dark eyes was lust, not love, and because Misty was a woman, she was in danger of reading too much into it.

Maybe he had done her a favour by kicking her out of his bedroom last night — destroying the last of her fantasies with one swift and cruel blow.

"It's going to be weird when it's all over," mused Lucas. "We'll have to work out some kind of plan."

"I've already got one," said Misty quickly. "I'll be leaving."

CHAPTER NINE

"Misty, I'm asking you to reconsider."

"Don't waste your breath, Gio."

Impatiently, Giovanni raked his fingers back through his thick, black hair, frowning as he took in the suitcases that were stacked next to the door along with a lamp, a box of books and a few other sundry items.

Misty wasn't just leaving for a holiday or a few days break while she went to collect her small son from his godmother's house in Cornwall. There in his hall lay the contents of the home she had made here for the past four years — the home that she was now planning to vacate.

"I can't see why you're doing this," he said stubbornly.

"Then you're not very perceptive."

"Why do women always talk in code?" he stormed.

"Because we stupidly believe that men have the emotional intelligence not to have everything spelled out for them!"

A nerve began to work in his cheek. "Look, Misty — just stay, will you?"

Misty shook her head. This was difficult enough. She was willing herself not to start blubbing, and he was making it even harder for her. But she knew that giving in to him would ultimately get her nowhere and she'd be right back where she started. Only worse.

Because now she had tasted intimacy with Giovanni. True, like the engagement itself it had only been a sham intimacy, but it still had the power to throw her emotions off-kilter and rock her whole world. And she needed to restore some calm again. Some order.

"I can't, Gio." She looked at him, her heart turning over and hoping it didn't show in her face. "You're too used to getting your own way. That's half your trouble."

Giovanni scowled, knowing that nothing had been right since the night he'd kicked her out of his bed. Because despite every effort in the book, he hadn't been able to wear her down and change her mind.

Misty had kept her resolve and resisted him, blocking every enticement to have sex with him again. For a man who had never known any kind of rejection from a woman, it had been a sobering lesson. But he had learned from it, hadn't he?

"I behaved thoughtlessly," he admitted, "for which I have apologized. So how long are you going to keep this up?'

"It isn't a game, Gio."

"You mean you're going to stay mad at me?"

"You're forgiven. Okay?"

"Then stay."

"No!" She sighed. "You must have realized all along that it would be impossible to go back to the way things were after all this."

"Just because of one night?"

Misty shook her head, the curls still loose and sun kissed. "That night has nothing to do with it. The world thinks that we're engaged to be married and soon that engagement is going to be broken, now that your step-sister is on the mend. Don't you think it's going to look rather odd if I slot back into my old position of housekeeper?"

"Who cares how it looks?" Giovanni demanded.

"I do. And it wouldn't feel right, either," she argued. "People would be bound to talk and to question me, and I don't want to be defined by my walk-on part in the life of Giovanni Cerruti." That's what she had been doing up until now, and she needed to be free of it. "How can I go back to serving you meals when I've shared them with you? How do you think it's going to feel when eventually you meet someone that you really do want to marry and I have to start taking orders from her? Don't you think that could be a little awkward?"

"I'm not planning on marrying *anyone*," he objected.

"Not now, you mean."

"Look, I'm not a great believer in happy-ever-after," he gritted. "I just know the house wouldn't be the same without you, Misty. And the sex is dynamic — you know it is." He shrugged as he slanted her a look of undiluted provocation. "Why stop something that we both enjoy so much?"

Misty stared at him in horror as his words reverberated around in her head like a bitter whirlwind. The sex is dynamic. Well, that told her exactly what her appeal to him was.

"What Gio wants, Gio gets — no matter what the cost to those around him. Or don't I count? Is that why you're so reluctant to let me go? Because having a 'relationship' with someone who works for you means that you're excused all the normal rules? You can treat me however the hell you like because you're paying me?"

Giovanni shook his head furiously. "How dare you talk to me this way. Other women would be bloody grateful to wear my ring and to be seen on my arm."

"Then go and make your delightful offer to one of *them*!" she stormed back. "I don't make good choices where men are concerned. I made a mistake with Dominic's father and I'm damned if I'm going to repeat it."

"And don't compare me to some waster who dumped you while you were pregnant!"

"You only want me because you can't have me, Giovanni," she said quietly. "Once you'd got me, you'd get bored and want to discard me."

And I can't risk that happening to me. Not with you. Not when it's so likely to happen. It would break her, and she could not afford to be broken — not with a child depending on her, as Dominic did.

Relationships were hard enough. But when there was such a fundamental inequality as that which existed between her and Giovanni, and he had emphatically told her that it was the sex that was great, which he didn't want to lose...

Well, that was just asking for trouble. Big trouble.

Like asking to have your heart broken.

"I'm leaving, Gio," she said. "And I mean it."

CHAPTER TEN

The beautiful redhead writhed against the sheets.

"Do it to me, Giovanni," she urged.

Giovanni froze in the act of unbuttoning his shirt. What the hell was he doing here? He stared at the naked beauty, knowing he didn't want her.

"I've made a mistake," he told her bitterly.

Outside, he stared up at an ink-black sky dotted with stars.

Every problem had a solution.

The question was whether he had the courage to use it.

He made himself wait until he was certain and the memory of the naked redhead had been erased from his mind. Then, that sleepless night, he climbed into his car and began the long drive to Cornwall.

A sound woke her.

In her remote cottage, Misty was used to hearing the caw of birds and the distant crash of the waves, but this sound was different. She looked at her watch and frowned. Three a.m.

Who was driving at this time of night?

Pulling on a velvet robe, she crept downstairs just as a car pulled up and there was a soft knock on the door. Her heart began to thunder even before she heard the distinctive voice.

"Misty?"

There was no point in playing games by ignoring him. She didn't want to wake Dom.

She opened the door, steeling her heart against the tall figure sillhouetted in the doorway — but she could do nothing to prevent its painful flutter of joy when she saw his shadowed face. "What are you doing here, Gio?" she whispered.

"Are you going to let me in?"

"What if I say no?"

"Go on. Say it then," he challenged, his eyes flinty in the moonlight.

Wordlessly, she pulled the door open and he stepped past her — strong, warm and virile. Her instinct was to touch him but she fought it. Give me strength, she prayed.

Giovanni walked into the tiny room where the embers of the fire still glowed. One of Dominic's drawings hung on the wall and there was a book open on the window seat.

It looked...

Giovanni swallowed. It looked like home.

He turned around. Her hair was loose and she wore blue velvet. Like a medieval painting come to life.

"Why are you here?" she questioned steadily.

"Why do you think?" He stared into her eyes and his heart turned over. What a fool he had been. "I miss you," he said softly.

Again, she steeled herself. She had to. "I'd be flattered if I thought there weren't other housekeepers just as capable as me," Misty answered coolly, "who can make your coffee the way you like it."

He stared at her incredulously. "Coffee? *Madre di Dio*! You think I've driven all this way to talk about coffee?"

"Is it the sex then?" she questioned. "Well, I'm sure the number of women waiting to step into my shoes on the sexual front is even greater." She made herself ask the question. "How many women since me, Giovanni?"

"None." There was a pause as Giovanni recognised that how he answered this was important. That only total honesty would do. "Other women don't work for me, any more," he admitted softly. "For the first time in my life I can only think about one...and that woman is you."

She bent to throw a log on the dying embers and then blew gently on the fire to start the blaze again. She wanted to believe him — so much — but she didn't dare let herself. For this time, Misty had much more to lose than her heart.

"You only want me because you haven't got me," she said quietly as she straightened up to meet his searching gaze. "I'm just another acquisition on the wish list of a man who has almost everything. Once you've got me, you'll get restless and want to move on. It's the way you are — it's the secret of your success, Giovanni."

"But that is where you're wrong, *cara mia*. Nothing is the same now you're gone." He had spent his life building fortunes and defying odds, but putting these feelings into words felt like the biggest mountain he'd ever had to climb. To survive as a child he'd learned to put up emotional barriers — which couldn't just come tumbling down overnight. He swallowed. "It felt so warm and easy when you were around, Misty. Everything is cold and empty now."

Her long hair shimmered as she gestured around her. "But I've built up a good life here. Dominic's happy at the local school and I have a job working at the local craft shop and I'm *good* at it. I don't need you, any more, Gio, don't you see that?"

"I don't want you to need me," he said softly. "I want you to want me — the way that I want you." His black eyes burned into her. "Do you want me, Misty? Because that's the only question that matters."

It was one of those defining moments.

She could turn him away and her life would be safe...yet Misty recognised it would also be empty and forever filled with an aching regret.

Or she could grab this unexpected chance of happiness, and take the risk that everyone had to take when they fell in love.

"Of course I want you," she whispered. "But I'm scared."

He laughed as he pulled her into his arms, closing his eyes as he breathed in the sweet scent of her hair. "You think I'm not? It's the reason I behaved so stupidly," he murmured. "But I recognise now that it's a healthy kind of scared. Like the first time you jump into water out of your depth — as long as you can swim, you'll be just fine." He tilted her chin and moved his lips close to hers. "Can you swim, Misty?"

She wound her arms around his neck. "Like a fish," she smiled, as she turned her face to his.

He bent and captured her mouth in a long kiss and in seconds she was trembling, robbed of everything but her desire for him.

"Gio?" she whispered unsteadily, as the flickering flames illuminated his dark features.

"Ssssh," he commanded, slipping the velvet robe from her bare shoulders. "Come here while I claim you."

"Th-that's a very old-fashioned thing to say," she stumbled.

He cupped her breast and touched his lips to it. "Sometimes old-fashioned is best."

And Misty wasn't going to argue with that. ▪

KRISSKROSS FILL-IN

4 letter words
Eggs
Grog
Leek
Mash
Miso
Sole
Stew

5 letter words
Icing
Limas
Noggs
Salad
Sushi

6 letter words
Cheese
Fondue
Grouse
Olives
Orange
Sesame
Stolen
Veggie

7 letter words
Eclairs
Giblets
Oatcake
Oysters
Sardine

8 letter words
Desserts
Scallops
Truffles

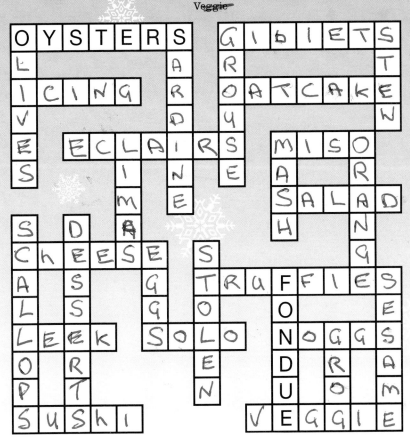

Romantic reads to
Need, Want

International affairs, seduction and passion guaranteed

8 brand-new books every month

From Regency England to Ancient Rome, rich, vivid and passionate romance...

3 brand-new books every month

Pulse-raising romance — heart-racing medical drama

6 brand-new books every month

Scorching hot sexy reads

4 brand-new books every month

Pure romance, pure emotion...

4 brand-new books every month

*Mills & Boon® books are available on the **first Friday of every month** from WHSmith, ASDA, Tesco and all good bookshops.*

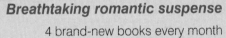

Puzzle Solutions

SU DOKU 1
PAGE 14

```
2 4 8 9 3 7 6 5 1
7 5 1 6 4 8 9 2 3
6 3 9 2 1 5 7 8 4
3 7 4 5 8 6 2 1 9
5 9 6 1 7 2 4 3 8
8 1 2 4 9 3 5 7 6
4 6 7 3 2 1 8 9 5
1 8 5 7 6 9 3 4 2
9 2 3 8 5 4 1 6 7
```

KAKURO
PAGE 15

GIANT CROSSWORD
PAGES 54-55

SU DOKU 2
PAGE 56

```
6 1 4 3 2 5 7 9 8
8 5 7 1 9 6 4 3 2
2 9 3 7 4 8 6 5 1
9 3 6 4 8 1 2 7 5
7 4 5 6 3 2 8 1 9
1 8 2 9 5 7 3 4 6
3 6 9 8 1 4 5 2 7
4 2 8 5 7 9 1 6 3
5 7 1 2 6 3 9 8 4
```

ARROW WORD
PAGE 57

HITORI
PAGE 87

```
7 7 6 6 1 1 1 3
4 3 8 2 1 5 6 7
2 8 6 8 7 2 4 5
1 8 7 7 2 2 2 4
7 8 3 5 4 8 1 1
1 4 1 2 2 2 7 8
6 5 7 4 3 7 4 1
3 5 7 1 1 4 5 3
```

WORDSEARCH
PAGE 107

CONNECT IT
PAGE 143

1 PORTHUMBROSNAN
2 ICINGIBSONOISY
3 REVAMPITTOPICS
4 BLOOMELODYACHT
5 BELIEFORDEMURE
6 TRIMEADOWILLIS
7 CONNERYOGAROMA
8 BALMUSICOSTNER